Behind the Now

by
Bob Freeman

Time Travel, but not like that

Behind the Now
by
Bob Freeman

Copyright © 2025 by Bob Freeman

First Edition published November 2025

Imprint: BtB Software, LLC

ISBN

        Paperback: 979-8-9905044-4-8
        Epub: 979-8-9905044-3-1

Library of Congress Control Number: 2025920809

Cover by:
Ghislain Viau
Creative Publishing Book Design
www. creativepublishingdesign. com

Edited by:
Eric Wyman
ecwyman @ gmail. com

Our Leader as a Pup

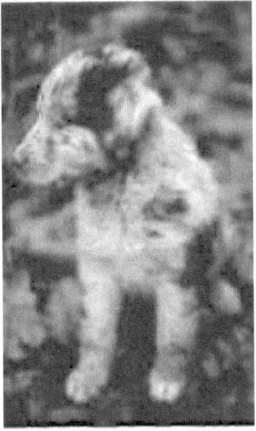

E=mc

Website>

IMDb>

Website: *www. h2liftship. com*

Socials: Please use
https:// www. H2liftship.com/contact
because who knows where the socials will be next week?

email: *SciFi @ h2liftship.com*

Disclaimer:
No AI's were used or hurt in production of this story.
Search engines, grammar/spell checkers, human editors
and artists all assisted in the final product.

Dedicated to all the dogs, Past, Present and Future
and support from Veronica for help beyond measure.

Earlier published short stories on this theme can be found here:
Time Slinky Novella published in Dark Horses -
The Magazine of Weird Fiction
'Time Jello' Published by scifiShorts.co

Behind the Now

by

Bob Freeman

Other books by the Author:

H$_2$LiftShips/

Contents

Time for an Introduction

Time is ubiquitous and in control.

We live in the Now, at Time's leading edge.

If we could send our robots to our galaxy's central black hole we might learn how Time twists. But we can't; it's far too distant and we don't have the time.

So what happens when Time passes? Do past actions continue to exist or are they only the collective memory of self, acquaintances, and our web of socials?

Throughout our collective artistic history, existing in sounds, books and video, we've visited the past using impossible time portals. The videos and books tell of elegant characters changing old Time and forcing the Now into an imaginary changed future. But that isn't how time travel works.

***

José never fit in with his peers. Raised by a stay-at-home mother and a mostly missing father in the Leave-It-To-Beaver suburbs, he was always the outlier.

In modern terms, he might be labeled as ADHD or PTSD or any other alphabet designation, but in his time he was just considered 'weird'. The label was a misappropriation of terms, as he was a science nerd and happy to display his badge to anyone who asked. Not that anyone ever did.

As befit his Mexican-Jewish heritage, he wasn't too tall, with curly black hair and a somewhat dark skin tone. He viewed life through intense brown eyes behind thick glasses with its bridge taped to hold the frame together. The white tape gave credence to his science-nerd credentials. It's not that he wanted to act the part of weird science kid, it's just that the cheap black rimmed glasses of the day broke a lot. His *tio* kept purchasing new frames for his *sobrino*, replacing every set until the next fracture.

José made it through high school with only a few physical bruises and fewer friends. Mentally he was intact, or at least had a shell that functioned in the regular world. But José didn't mind being out of step with his classmates. It gave him time to think for himself.

Time and its movements were the driving force of his life. He would prefer to explore time at the edge of black holes, where matter and time take on different properties, but that wasn't an option. Location both limited and directed his line of inquiry. He was, after all, nothing more than a human standing on a tiny wet rock spinning along with a middle-aged third-rate star at the edge of a spiral galaxy. He had no way to travel the vast distances required to reach a black hole.

The problem was, again, time. There wasn't enough of it in the relatively short span he was afforded in order to accomplish his goals. The fact that crossing an accretion disk's time dilation would probably end his consciousness was a problem he would not have to address. He simply couldn't get there from here.

The world he lived on, and the historical difficulty of leaving it, helped keep him alive. If he had something better than the wimpy kerosene/oxygen-powered rockets, he might have a chance to test his theories. Only the rich, the well-placed, or the military elites could use those puny, slow, farty transports. FasterThanLight or Warp drives would help, but he couldn't use fantasy rockets for his experiments, no matter how popular they were in comic books and movies. He was forever Earth-bound and unable to test his killer ideas off-planet.

It was a long and tedious path to this point in time for José Isaac Davidovich, TimeWall Explorer. He didn't spring fully clothed from the head of Zeus or any other entity, but instead made his way in the world as a human sentient. He was a normal child, as normal as any glasses-wearing, skinny, slightly OCD kid could be anyway.

Quiet noises led José on his path of discovery. Poor vision enhanced his hearing in his exploration of the world. He wasn't a bat, but he had a habit of humming as he walked, sound gently bouncing off obstacles to ensure he wouldn't bump against too many walls. Echoes of soft singing, sounding like gentle banshee songs, answered his toneless tunes. He received questioning glances from other humans, but birds, rabbits, and other beasts listened to the sounds and responded on the same wavelength.

He was a member of a typical nuclear family; mother, father, and relatives. His mother did her best to guide her only son, but his unrelenting OCD and intelligence could be a burden even with a functional family. For his mother, it was difficult to enforce society's concept of normality on a child who chose his own path. His father dealt with his unusual son by spending most of his time away. He supported his family in his own way, but left interactions with his son to his brother, José's *tio* Carlos, the professor.

His candy-apple red bicycle became José's constant companion. It arrived one day in a box, unassembled, as a present from his father who couldn't seem to make it home for the winter holidays. Maybe his papa's eighteen-wheeler was in some distant part of the country delivering packages to warehouses, or he was a scientist working in a secret underground lair. Or more likely, he just didn't care to be at home with his weird kid. It was an expensive present, if paid for, and became a puzzle for José to assemble. José spent hours in the basement, tinkering with the bike until it was his reliable warhorse to escape the seemingly unending stream of suggestions his mother insisted on sharing.

In a world where the automobile was king, a kid spinning through the neighborhoods wasn't unusual, but somehow José made it a gossip-able feature. José didn't care about norms. With his dark curls flying, he passed blurred houses, people, and cars which became his world to explore and not crash into. Traveling north, he could break away to the surrounding foothills, struggling through the gears up the winding roads and flying back down, brakes smoking on the sharp curves.

3

The bike became his introduction to mechanics, and the wind blasting down the road enhanced the banshee singing he couldn't seem to shake. As fast as he traveled down the hills, Time was always with him and there was no mechanical way to break through the barrier. His bike was frequently found at the front door of the local library, where science fiction books became his next obsession, teaching him about things beyond time and this planet. A copy of Popular Science led to his exploration of crystal radios and began his investigation of all things electronic, while never forgetting his goal of exploring Time.

He wasn't trying to escape the present, but once José latched onto a concept, it became over-reaching. His unending goal was to learn all he could about Time, if only for the fun of exploring new methods and building devices that no one else had considered.

Chapter 01 -
Time for Family

It was the end of summer and cool enough to spend some time outside before the cold bite of winter sent the insects into a deep sleep.

"José," shouted his mother, "Get the tablecloth and make sure the edges are secure. It's windy today."

José gathered up the plates and glasses and carefully walked down the outside steps.

"Is my *Tio* Carlos coming too?" asked José.

"Of course," said Lara. "I hope he's not going to bring another one of his janky girlfriends."

"It's fine with me," said Irving. "I don't mind his girlfriends, he's still single, you know."

Lara replied with a look and a glare.

"Don't forget a place setting for your *tia* Rose. She promised to come. I've invited our new neighbors, too. They have a kid your age. You need to make friends."

"That's just great," said Irv. "I didn't buy enough carne to feed the neighbors and your sister. She had better not bring her yappy little dog. It's no bigger than a rat and acts like one, too."

"I like him, he's friendly," said José.

"That works for you, son," said Irv. "He doesn't like me and it's mutual. Lara, who are these neighbors? Why didn't you tell me about them? Are we supposed to feed the whole block? They better bring food."

Lara ignored the rant as best she could.

"It's only two more people, Mrs. Smith and her son Hector, she just lost her husband and is new to the neighborhood.

"Sorry to hear that," said Irv. "It doesn't change the equation. We have more people here today than food."

"I've made a pot of beans and there's enough corn for everyone," said Lara.

"Great. Now we get to eat cow and what they eat too."

"Irv, we need to have company. The boy is alone, what with you traveling for weeks on end. We'll be fine."

Carlos and Irv turned to the BBQ, a can of flammable liquid nearby in case of emergencies.

"At least the wind will keep the bugs down," said Carlos. "Maybe we won't get bitten by too many mosquitoes this time."

"It's the chiggers I hate, but don't worry, I've got that covered," claimed Irv. "I sprayed the whole backyard with that new product, DDT. Have you heard of it at the university?"

"Not specifically," said Carlos. "I've barely started the program. I'm still trying to pick a major."

"So, not chemical engineering or agriculture from the sound of it?" said Lara.

"Those are options, yes. I'm in the science department," said Carlos. "There are a lot of programs to choose from."

Lara leaned over to José, "Please stop humming and listen to what your *tio* is saying, you need think of your future."

José lowered the volume to an internal hum and tuned into the conversation. His hearing was superb, almost to canine level. He had almost too much input and humming was his way to filter out the fluff.

"The Time lab is just starting up," said Carlos, "I might look into it."

"What do they do?" said Lara. "Is it like the movies? Can you change our history?"

"Cool," whispered José. "*Tio* Carlos. What do they study? Can I help you?"

"Now José, you'll have to wait to go to college. There are years of work in front of you. First you have to finish high school. Let's not try to jump the line, you'll have to pay your dues, like everyone else."

"But time travel, *Tio* Carlos!" exclaimed José. "I've always been interested in Time. I think I know where it comes from. Let me write down some ideas you can give the head of the department."

"The professor who heads the TimeLab? Dr. Jamienson? I think not. I've heard too many bad things about her. It's almost like being in the Army."

"I thought everything was fun and easy in college," said Irving. "Isn't that why you're going instead of working like the rest of us?"

Carlos retorted, "I may take some courses in the Time group, but there is no way I'd work in that department as long as she's in charge. I heard she once threw a student out a window."

"That's shocking," said Lara. "How is she still allowed to work there?"

"She brings in a lot of money to the university," said Carlos. "It didn't cause any harm. It was winter and the snowbank caught him. No damage, no repercussions."

"Tell you what," said Irv. "If college is so bad, you can join me on my next trip. You'd be a natural in my line of work. I can give you a good reference."

Lara said, "or join the Army, like Irv did. They will even pay for higher education."

Irving took a long sip from his beer and turned the carne asada on the barbecue. He wasn't interested in going down the path of higher education or being reminded of that option.

José broke into the conversation, "I know what you can do, *Tio.* You can invent a time machine and go back and replace the professor."

Irving finally came up with a rejoinder, since it didn't look like his wife was going to defend him.

"Hey," said Irv. "What's wrong with the Army? I served and so should you, instead of hiding in a school."

"I'm not hiding, I'm expending my resources in a different direction. Anyhow, I don't think time travel is what the Time Lab is trying to do," said Carlos.

"Well, that's what the TV shows," said Lara.

"That's right," said Carlos. "I heard that the *Captain Z-Ro* show is now on our local station."

"That must have been what I saw on TV," said Lara. "I'm sure glad that those dedicated Time Travelers are willing to risk their lives to fix history."

Irv followed the conversation like a tennis match. He didn't have anything to add; drinking his beer before it got warm seemed more important.

TV was something he knew about.

"I saw that show," said Irving. "It doesn't look like messing with Time is a good thing. What if they made a mistake?"

"I agree," said Lara. "You shouldn't play around with the forces of nature."

"I'm sure the university's TimeLab is nothing like TV. The school's brochure says they are looking at the force and structure of energy, and Time is just another energy source."

"So, a weapon," said Irv. "I'm not surprised. The government is always looking for new weapons."

"The TV shows are only concerned with excitement," said Carlos. "I'm sure studying Time is very boring.

"I always wondered what's behind Time," said José. "Did you know that the time-banshees sing to me? I put together a prototype machine that may help me talk to them. Can you take me to the TimeLab? I'm sure they would want to see my device."

Lara shook her head while Carlos looked for an easy way out of this discussion.

Irv kept to the BBQ and beer as he looked to Carlos's latest girlfriend for encouragement.

"I'm sure it works fine. You can show it to me later," said Carlos, "I haven't even picked my courses for this year. I don't think I can bring you to that or any other lab right now."

Jose was crestfallen. Another dream delayed.

"Let me tell you," said Lara, "There's nothing good that can come with messing with Time."

"You certainly don't want to go back in time unsupervised," said Carlos. "There might be monsters. I bet you'd find *LaLlorona* and a *Chupacabra* or two, and who knows what else?"

"Shh," said Lara. "Don't talk to the boy about those *monstruos* behind Time. It will just scare him. He barely sleeps now as it is. I don't want you to bring up that subject ever again."

"Yes, Lara," said Carlos.

Irving leaned over and whispered, "Now you know what I have to deal with; it's no wonder I like to travel."

"Hush," said Lara. "The neighbors are here. José, please don't talk about your toys."

"We brought dessert, your BBQ smells delicious," said Mrs. Smith.

Chapter 02 -
Time to Show Off

Mrs. Smith and her son Hector sat down at the picnic table. "We brought a lime Jello mold. It has bananas in it."

"Thanks," said Lara. "Please put it on the table and we'll have it for dessert."

Mrs. Smith said "I've never seen flank steak used on a barbecue. Is that a cultural thing?"

"That's right," said Irv. "We try to draw from all cultures."

"Even the Indians?" said Hector. "They were here first."

"Well, maybe not," said Lara.

"Hector," said Mrs. Smith. "Mind your manners."

She turned to Lara, "The kid loves to study history, maybe a bit too much."

"But let's eat," said Lara. "We have mild hot sauce for you if you'd prefer it over our regular fare."

"Ketchup?" asked Hector.

José snorted, "No one uses ketchup on carne asada burritos. Even I know that."

In spite of the rough start and a few more *faux pas*, food took precedent, even the beans.

Irv turned to Lara and whispered, "We're running out of carne. Those kids eat like they have a hole in their stomachs. We need to cut them off."

"They're growing boys, Irv. Of course they're going to have appetites. Even José is on his second burrito."

"Well, it might put some meat on his bones. But it won't help if there's nothing left to eat."

Lara turned to the two boys and said, "José, take Hector to your play room and show him your latest toy."

"Mother!" exclaimed José. "It's not a play room, it's my lab. And it isn't a toy."

Lara looked at her guests and smiled, "He likes to call his play room a laboratory, isn't that cute?"

"Is it dangerous?"

"No, it's only a bunch of tools and old TVs. Perfectly harmless."

"Hector, go with your new friend," said Mrs. Smith.

"Can't we go home, Mom?" said Hector.

"The adults want to talk some more," said Mrs. Smith. "Go play with your new friend."

"Neighbor," said Hector.

"Don't sass me, young man."

"The kids will be fine," said Lara. "Irv, grab some more beer from the house."

Hector sighed. "Okay Mom." Without more food and nothing but adults talking, playing with toys was the best alternative.

"So tell me, Lara, are you renting this house?"

"We've been here for years, if you must know," said Lara. "My parents bought this place and it's mine now."

"*Our* house," said Irving.

No food and more beer was bound to make the adult conversation fly. The two boys wisely made it back to the house.

The entrance to José's 'play-room' was through the kitchen past a thin plywood door hung on cheap hinges. A pull handle led to steep stairs. A single light shone on the stairs leading to José's private space.

"This is cool," said Hector. "Our basement is filled with old clothes and discarded toys."

"My parents don't like to come down here. My mother is afraid of the steep stairs and my papa is busy with work. I cleaned and organized everything back to the bare walls."

On an old hollow-core door, serving as a workbench, José had the guts of a couple of TVs, a soldering iron and assorted electronic devices.

"Your parents let you have a soldering iron? Cool," said Hector.

"My uncle gave it to me. He's a freshman at the university."

"That isn't for me. I'm going to go into the Army or Marines when I graduate high school. I'm already tired of school."

"After one year?" said José. "I've always looked forward to high school and college. I want to learn all I can about everything."

"Good luck with that," said Hector. "What are you working on?"

Hardly anyone asked José about his passions and this was his time to shine.

He stammered, "A time device."

Hector didn't back away and José continued, "My uncle told me about the university's Time Lab and I want to work there."

"Time, huh? I guess that would be fun. How does it work?"

José said. "It doesn't yet, but I'm getting closer. See the vacuum tubes? I de-tune them to resonate at the banshee's frequencies to crack open Time."

Hector started to back away. "Banshee frequencies? What's that?"

"It's Banshee singing leaking through the TimeWall. Didn't you know that?"

Hector took another step back.

"No, I can't say that I've heard those. Do they sound anything like the big rigs on the interstate?"

"Well, they are sounds. Not as guttural as a truck. I thought everyone knew about it. That's why I hum sometimes, to drown them out. How do you handle it?"

"What?" said Hector. "I don't hear anything and I'm not sure I want to."

"I can show you. My device amplifies those sounds and shoots them back at the TimeWall."

"That's interesting," said Hector, stepping a little closer.

"My mother doesn't like me to blast out the sounds when people are around. I'll turn it on for you, but I have to keep it low."

The machine warmed up, vacuum tubes igniting, as a low wail came out of the speakers.

"Wait. I do hear something. I think it's my mother. I have to go."

"Hang on a minute. Let me give the amplifier a boost. You'll love this sound."

11

Sure enough, sounds started blasting out the re-purposed TV speakers. The vacuum tubes began to glow purple.

"Are those tubes going to explode?" asked Hector. "I thought you told my mother this wasn't going to be dangerous."

"Don't worry, I'm watching the output. Just listen to what they have to say."

"Are they like the Greek Sirens? I read about them in class. I wouldn't mind meeting them. They don't wear shirts."

"I can show you more later if you want," said José.

"I'll let you know," said Hector. "I've got to go."

José turned down the dial and the song drifted off, much to the irritation of the Banshees.

Chapter 03 -
Time for Papa

José was lying in his bed, sorting through the noises of the night as the burritos settled in his stomach.

The sound of crickets, the occasional raccoon, field mice, and the whoosh of owls looking for their nightly breakfast filled the air. The banshees were always in the background, a song he couldn't escape. Cars and long-haul trucks on the distant interstate were a constant low rumble that tied the sounds together.

José wasn't afraid of the banshee wails, and cryptids seldom bothered to bang on his bedroom door, begging for entertainment and blood.

He concentrated on the symphony of the night, ignoring the overly loud discussions in the other room.

The guest bedroom was a buffer between José and his parents' room. Irv was using it to store his samples and travel gear. No matter how much material was in the room, it only sucked up a few decibels of the adult discussions of Lara and Irving.

Between the hushed arguments of his parents and the distant banshee wails, there was a new sound that got his attention. The scratching on his bedroom door couldn't be ignored. José thought, *Do we have mice again? I hope Papa doesn't ask me to help him trap them. I'm sure he wouldn't want to know I've been keeping them as pets.*

José stirred from his warm bed. *Should I check? What if it's a real monster? I don't want to deal with it tonight!*

A whimper and a squeak at the bedroom door added to the concert.

That's not a monster. "Paquito. What are you doing here? Are they arguing again?"

Paquito couldn't answer, at least not in English. He wagged his tail and jumped onto José's bed

"Okay. I guess you want to stay here tonight? I can't blame you. It's getting a bit loud over there."

Words made their way from the private sanctum of his parents' bedroom and couldn't be ignored.

"All I'm saying, Lara, is that the kid needs some help."

"Irv, he's your son, and my baby boy. You can't just toss him out because he doesn't blend in with the other kids."

"Blend in? He can't even play ball. It's embarrassing to see him wince and drop the ball. Don't even get me started on the way he throws."

"Don't blame the kid. He's still getting used to wearing glasses."

"What do you mean? He's been wearing glasses for over 10 years."

"Thirteen. You don't even know how old he is."

"Okay. Thirteen. Forgive me, I have to spend a lot of time on the road. How else can we make a living?"

"Sorry, dear, I know you work hard for us."

Irving accepted the compliment, no matter how forced.

In this family, an argument only ends when Lara says it does. She said, "Please don't criticize my boy. He's doing the best with what he has. They've tested him at school and he's not dumb."

"Well, he needs a haircut," said Irving.

"Leave his hair out of it. All the kids wear it long. Don't you want him to fit in?"

"With a bunch of beatniks and losers? No. That's why I think we should send him to one of those military camps this year. It will set him straight."

"He's too young and fragile. The school counselor said he might be an almost-genius. You can't send a genius to a military school."

"Genius my ass. I never graduated high school and look how successful we are!"

"In the house I inherited?"

Irv let that sink in and quietly stewed.

"Okay. I see where this is going. I have to leave early. We can talk about it when I get back. I have a job starting upstate. I'll be back in a few weeks."

Lara wasn't ready to let Irv off so easy. "That's why the boy is confused. He loves his Papa and you're never home."

"I have to work. Where do you think our food comes from?"

"Fine."

"Fine. I'm going to sleep in the guest room. I still have to pack and I'll be up at 4am. Please join me for breakfast, let the boy get his beauty sleep."

José heard the conversation and ignored the words.

Paquito heard the vibes and buried deeper into the covers.

Slamming doors and silence told José and Paquito that the almost nightly discussions were over. Paquito sighed and quickly fell asleep. Chihuahua snoring blending into the night.

José did his best to get back to his normal sleep routine, although lately, it seemed that arguments were becoming way too normal.

The smell of fresh Spam® and potatoes grilling in the kitchen dragged José out of bed.

Paquito had already left at the sound of a can opening.

The guest room door was open, the bed left unmade. José walked by, looked in and shrugged.

"Where's Papa, *Madre*? I was going to show him my latest experiments."

Lara said nothing but placed a plate of fresh Spam® burritos in front of José.

She stood there, facing the stove as he ate, then said, "Your papa had to get up early. He has a job upstate and needed to leave."

"Will he be back soon? I've made some modifications in my device and I'm sure he'd like to see them."

Lara didn't answer the question and said, "He said he was sorry to miss seeing your toy, but he'll be happy to check it out when he gets back. Now get ready for school. I made some tuna-fish sandwiches and there are some Fig Newtons in the cabinet."

Chapter 04 -
Time for a Basement

José was a bit of a pack rat. Anything unwanted or unloved from his high school shop class would invariably migrate to his basement workshop.

His playthings were discarded TVs, stripped for parts with vacuum tubes and mechanical comb-rheostats piled on his shelf. No matter what he was working on, he couldn't ignore the sounds escaping from the house's rock-wall foundation, whispering their songs of ancient history.

He listened to the rocks and was determined to find out what else they had to say. Amplifiers were easy to build, rocks connected with a metal stethoscope transmitting deep, slow tunes he could sample and few others could hear.

"Maybe the rocks can teach me about Time?" said José. There was no one else to talk to, but he knew the stones would understand.

His mother stood at the top of the basement stairs, worried about what her only son was becoming. *I wish Irving was here*, she thought. *He could talk to his boy. Maybe he could tell him about his job and pique his interest in the outside world. Whatever devil device José's building can't be good. No one is supposed to talk to rocks.*

José didn't notice his mother, not that he could explain what he was doing if he had. Unless there was food involved, the two seldom talked.

"José, I made you a tuna sandwich," his mother called out. "Hurry up or I'll feed it to the dog. I've found the rye bread you like."

"Is it the one with extra caraway seeds? Don't let Paquito eat it, the seeds don't agree with him. I'll be right there, I'm on to something and only have to record my samples before I can play them back."

"You aren't going to make noise again, I hope? Some of the neighbors are beginning to talk and it makes the dog howl."

"What do you mean?" said José. "That little Chihuahua loves my work, that's why he sings along."

"He hides under the bed. It hurts his ears."

"Fine, I'll make him some noise-canceling headphones. What color do you think he likes?"

His mother shook her head. *Why does he want to torture my poor dog?* "He doesn't need headphones, just make less noise."

"Sorry Mom. I'm sure the neighbors will understand, once I get my Time Machine working.

"Please don't mention that word to my friends. It's crazy talk. Now come up to the kitchen. I'll get you some cold milk to go with your sandwich."

"I'll be right up. Don't worry. You'll be proud of me once this is finished."

"Finish quietly, please," said his mother.

José jammed a flat metal rod in an exposed rock joint and connected it with alligator clips to feed the signal into an old CRT acting as an oscilloscope.

"Sorry, my friends, I hope this doesn't hurt," said José.

If there were any replies, José would see them, displayed as long-range sound waves, logarithmically compressed. The signal was then tweaked and boosted into frequencies closer to what most humans could hear. José, with his sensitive, wide-ranging hearing could pick up the sounds in dog-adjacent signals.

"It would be interesting to see if I could talk to the rocks, but what would I say? Can they even relate to us? We're soft-bodied cellular beings, and they're minerals. I bet we look like wraiths to them, zipping around as they sit connected to the Earth."

The rocks didn't answer his questions, appearing inert to the living cells that were embodied in the person called José.

"Well, that's a project for a different day. I still need to test the gear and see if I can bring up the TimeWall."

José began tweaking the rock's tones, building up the amplitude to tease out Time, trying to make it stand still and show itself. It wasn't the sound of pure crystals, but rough minerals singing the songs of their existence.

"I know my mother asked me not to make a lot of noise, but it'll be a short trial. I'm sure she won't mind. It's for science, after all."

He ran the signals through a series of vacuum tubes, rapidly glowing in electronic excitation. Grabbing the dial of a rheostat, he adjusted the signal to blend rock talk to aural frequencies. The lab was bathed in the light of vacuum tubes glowing purple, giving the old black and white CRT screen a sickly color. All the scenario needed was for José to laugh manically to complete the picture. But he failed to see the humor and instead concentrated on the intersection of the world and sounds where a coin-sized apparition bubbled and glowed in response.

"That's it!" exclaimed José. "I'm sure that's a piece of the TimeWall. It's a little small, but I can work on that."

A rapping noise, rhythmic to start and then more random began to interfere.

"I hope it isn't going to explode."

José turned off the device and the generated sounds slowly dissipated.

The pattern emanating from the basement's ceiling became regular, then stopped.

"I told you no noise!" shouted his mother. "Come up and eat your lunch before I toss it out."

The pattern was now obvious, a broom handle tapping above his head.

"Yes, *Madre*, I was just running a simple test. I'll be right there."

"'Simple' my ass," his mother said under her breath. "That boy will be the death of me. He needs a good talking to. He needs his father here."

José locked the basement door behind him. Not that anyone would enter his laboratory sanctuary. Its residue sounds of banshees were ready to confront all who entered.

"I made the tuna fish sandwich just the way you like it. One tablespoon of mayonnaise on fresh rye bread and a jalapeño pepper cut in small pieces with the seeds removed."

"*Gracias.* You always know what I like."

"That's my boy. I'm making baked chicken and potato pancakes for dinner."

"What's the occasion? A celebration? Is Papa coming home tonight?"

"No. I just thought it would be nice to have a good home-cooked meal."

"Okay," said José, a little disappointed. "Too bad Papa won't be here."

"I'm sure he'll be back soon," said his mother. "Maybe you can show him your noise machine. I'm sure he'll come by this summer."

José said, "That's okay. I'm going to test my machine tomorrow morning."

"Please don't wake the neighbors. They might call the police if it's too early."

"Don't worry, I'll take my bike and ride to the foothills, away from everyone."

"Well, at least you'll be outside getting some exercise instead of stuck in that cold dark basement. I'll pack you a lunch. Is tuna okay?"

Tuna fish again! thought José. *I'm surprised there is any tuna left in the sea.*

"It's fine," he replied.

"I've got some Fig Newtons, too. And don't forget to take water. And a warm coat."

"Yes, *Madre*," said José. "I'm going to get my gear ready. I promise to be quiet."

"Thank you. I'm going to bed, I've got a headache. I'll leave your clothes out for you.

Chapter 05 -
Time for a Trial

José was wrapped in the oversized trench coat his mother insisted he wear to ward off the morning chill. She found it abandoned in the guest closet, forgotten when his papa left for his last job. With the exception of his backpack, with its array of speakers and sensors, he could almost be mistaken for one of the many hikers traveling the trails.

José looked around, almost wanting validation of his experiments, but he found himself alone, breathing heavily from the walk in the wet grass and in anticipation of testing out his theories. He adjusted his glasses; black frames with classic white tape on the bridge. José wore his nerd badge with pride, at least until a new unbroken pair was ready.

Time to give it a try, thought José, without a hint of irony. He connected the battery and warmed up his latest experiment, pointing the speakers at the grassy folds marching up the round hills. Capacitors charged up as vacuum tubes lent an eerie glow to the surroundings. José admired his handiwork, looking for the signs of overheated electronics. *Well, nothing is smoking so far*, he thought as he increased the amperage.

A hum, becoming a crescendo of noise, resembling sound, wailed from his backpack. The hairs on his arms rose as air itself noticed, stood at attention, and waited. Molecules, microbes, dirt, and insects became trapped in the focused sound explosion he created. Quantum interactions sparkled as Time made its presence known as a multi-polarized, undulating, bubbling flicker. Flashing strings of energy tied the wall together.

"There it is," whispered José, almost afraid of breaking the spell. "I'm sure that's the TimeWall, and those strings must be quantum bits connecting it all."

His DIY contraption produced no pressure wave but acted on the QTmBit level to bind with Time on its own plane. The imitation banshees emanating from his backpack woke up Time and made it dance to their tune.

The TimeWall was unclimbable, filling the Universe with its rhythm in the place we call the world. Time's leading edge shimmered and twisted, pieces forming into shiny, colored opportunity blobs pulsing to the beat of the ages before dissolving into the background.

Time was unconcerned. The odds of being trapped by this sentient's boom-box were a simple infinite integral approaching zero. Showing itself to the Now was unusual but not beyond the limits of Time's experience.

The wall appeared immutable and empty simultaneously. Time waited. It was in no rush to meet José, one moment was as good as another. The wall was frozen in his sound trap, and it was up to José to make the next move.

José stepped forward, mere millimeters in front of the transitory structure called Time. The banshees and stretched ions screaming from his backpack kept the wall visible.

He stopped.

Moving forward meant forcing his way through the pulsing apparition.

José secured his goggles and twisted the lenses, adjusting filters and bringing the barrier into sharper focus. He didn't know what would happen once he passed through the TimeWall. His custom eyewear was the only protection he had against dangerous optical repercussions. If worse came to worst, he wasn't dependent on sight and could maneuver using the numerous sensors pinging away in his backpack. Scientific advancement involves risk, but he did enjoy seeing and had no desire to lose that function in the transaction.

One of his leading sensors disappeared in the standing wave. He glanced at the display and saw nothing but gray streaks. Thoughts raced. *If this is what is behind the TimeWall, I'm in for a world of hurt.*

His biggest fear was disintegration, one qubit at a time. Another thought crossed his mind, echoing like a dropped ping-pong ball. *Would I cease to exist without Time binding my molecules to Now's plane of existence?*

José whispered, "This is what I've been waiting for. No backing out now."

His stated worries were no more than a dry whiff against the howling sounds.

To be the first to stand behind the TimeWall was all he ever wanted.

He was a self-taught time-scientist, and the pursuit of knowledge was worth practically any risk. At worst, he would join in an unwelcome sing-along with the banshee sounds blasting from his backpack. No one would know the difference as he was pulled apart bit by bit behind Time's leading edge.

Even with thoughts of his dissolution, he had a plan. He set up a video camera he found abandoned in an old storage box. It would record everything on a Sony Betamax® video cassette. It didn't bother him that a classic movie would give up its ghost to science, but his mother might have had different ideas.

The leading edge of Time passed over, under, and through everything in its path. A bubble pooched out, touched noses, and raced up his face at the speed of time. Thinner than a boson, a QTmBit, connected to totality and nothing at all was Time's leading edge. José's nose tingled.

He crossed his eyes, glanced down, and thought, *Whew, the tip of my nose is still there. Maybe there's a chance this can work!*

Time was not consistent, especially when trifled with at close range. Time bubbles pulled and pushed at his body, giving tit for tat for his insolence. Time was determined to remind the intruder that it was in control and Time was the only thing that mattered. José was hit with blows, twisting his insides and unsynching cells as the TimeWall marched to the Now. It took a while until his guts re-stabilized, and weak knees, headache, and nausea were signs of success.

Would he be able to move around in the past, changing the future or forcing a new path? Only time would tell, he thought with a chuckle. The wall moved on, no longer part of his reality. Sensations of dread from behind the TimeWall enveloped José as he became wrapped up in the odors of mold and decay where past became present.

Despite Time's rude welcome, José was unfazed; twisted guts and short-circuited neurons wouldn't stop his quest. His TimeWall-breaking backpack was not as lucky. Quantum changes flipped diodes and overloaded capacitors. The vacuum tubes he salvaged from an old TV began overheating, purple electrons spanning toward ultraviolet and beyond.

As the wall passed and Time became the Now, his nausea settled. "Uh-oh," whispered José as his backpack smoked, the acrid smell of overheated capacitors standing in for the diminishing banshee shouts.

José sat down hard. The deadman's switch dropped, and his concert slowly ran down, like a bagpipe losing steam.

I need a break, thought José. *I wonder if my madre packed any surprise treats in my lunch bag? I think my equipment needs a cool down, too."*

José didn't have a lunch box splashed with action heroes or outer space themes. Not that he didn't own a few of those, but he made due with a brown bag filled with cookies and half a leftover tuna sandwich.

There was no one to talk to, but talking out loud helped him think and it certainly didn't seem any stranger than a kid facing grass-covered foothills blasting screams to the world.

José glanced at his watch, a present from his *tio* on his 13th birthday, and said, "It took a licking and kept on ticking." An old joke, but somehow appropriate. He forgot to check the start time of his experiment and had no idea if he spent seconds or hours in Time's embrace.

He checked the backpack and munched on cookies, looking for blown electronics or melted connections. Without spending hours with a multimeter to confirm viability, José shrugged and said, "That was interesting. Everything looks reasonably intact, and I think there's enough juice left to try another run."

José flipped the power switch, the machine sputtered, vacuum tubes barely glowed and a capacitor smoked and melted.

He continued the dialog with the absent TimeWall, "I guess I'm done for the day, but at least everything worked. I'd better add some more capacitors to handle the load and replace the batteries. I wonder if RadioShack™ is open today?"

Chapter 06 -
Time for Breakfast

José sped down the path on his bicycle, his backpack tightly strapped to the rear fender rack. He flew past the cemetery and quickly passed through the center of town. The trip up the narrow, twisting road to his isolated testing site was rugged, but coming back was easy; all downhill.

He thought, *maybe his mother could make him some of his favorite breakfast burritos, with Spam®.*

He peddled up the driveway to the isolated bungalow his family called home.

I'm in luck, thought José. *It doesn't look like my mother is up. I'll just sneak in through the garage and stash my gear. Maybe my papa is back in town. I'm sure he'd want to hear of my successful test.*

He quietly turned the garage door handle and lifted the door. Squeaky springs announced his entrance back to the Now world. "I should have lubricated the springs. Don't know how I missed that when I was working on my bike."

Paquito watched as José approached and ran down to greet him.

"Quiet Paquito, I don't want to wake anyone."

Paquito slowly wagged his tail, showing acceptance of the rules of engagement.

José ran his hand over the frame, and said to Paquito, "I hope my bike is okay. I thought I heard a pebble hit the down-tube on the last hairpin turn. I'm running low on touch-up paint. It better not be a big ding."

Paquito followed, sniffing and checking every stage of the inspection.

José, true to his compulsive behavior, wiped down the bike with a rag and some WD-40® and placed the backpack carefully on his workbench.

He ran his hand over the offending bike tube, but if there was a ding, no one else would notice.

"I guess the bike is undamaged. I'll unpack later," said José. "I need some food first. The recordings can wait until after breakfast."

He heard the sound of a car in the driveway. "Is that my Papa, back from his business trip?" said José. "I wonder if he found the octal socket for the vacuum tubes I asked for? I hope he can stay for my birthday. We could have a party."

The car was a racing-green Triumph Roadster, not something his father would drive. "It's my *tio*. I wonder what he wants? I hope my *madre* made enough breakfast for all of us."

His *tio* parked and knocked once before entering the kitchen where José's mother was brewing coffee.

"Carlos," said Lara. "I'm glad you came. José left early, before dawn, and I didn't know where he was going. I think he's dealing drugs."

"Drugs? Now, now, Lara. I'm sure there is a valid reason for what he's doing," said Carlos. "Maybe he's collecting bugs. He did that a lot when he was younger."

"I think I saw him in the driveway before you drove up," said Lara. "He was trying to sneak in, I'm sure of it. Was he out all night with a girlfriend? Or maybe he was doing something worse?"

"Why don't we simply ask him before jumping to conclusions. Let me talk to him, *mano e mano*."

"I wish your brother was here. He knows how to talk to his boy."

Carlos said nothing. Lara's husband seemed to be at home less and less over the years and discussions on his whereabouts were often a sore point with his sister-in-law.

"I know it's his busy time and once winter sets in, he can park his rig and help with José," said Lara.

"I'm sure he'll be back soon," said Carlos. "My brother has always been a wanderer, but he always comes back home."

Lara exclaimed, "Look! José just wheeled his bicycle into the garage. Did you see him covered with grass and mud? What was he doing out so early, sneaking out of the house with his weird toys? Is he making a bomb? Something's wrong with my husband's child."

"Don't worry, Lara," said Tio Carlos. "He's just a boy, going through some growing pains."

"He better not be using those psycho drugs my book club mentioned. Some of the other parents are having horrible times with their kids. One poor woman found out that her dear sweet child ate a mushroom and almost died."

Carlos tut-tutted in agreement.

"Tell me," said Lara. "Who would go out in the forest and chew on some unknown mushroom? That's just sick. I've heard about these wild beatnik cults that do it."

Carlos poured some cream into his coffee, waiting for Lara to find a different topic.

"Can you ask him if he's in a cult, or meeting up with beatniks?"

"I'll bring that up when I talk to him after breakfast," said Carlos.

Carlos wasn't having any luck guiding the conversation as José's mother revisited her favorite theme.

"I wish his father was here. He needs a strong hand to guide him."

"Tell you what," said Carlos. "I just finished some programming for the bus company and they gave me a three-month travel pass as a bonus. How about we let José see a bit of the world, maybe visit his cousins?"

"I don't know," said Lara. "Will he be safe, traveling alone? The boy's barely sixteen."

"Of course he'll be safe. He'll have a bus pass. He needs to learn to take care of himself. Don't worry, buses go to the center of most towns and those are some of the safest places to visit, I've heard. He can get on and off anytime he wants."

"Maybe he'll make some friends on the road," said Lara. "Are you sure buses are dependable? It isn't like riding the rails or hitchhiking, is it?

"Just think," said Carlos. "You'll have the whole house to yourself for a few months while José is learning how to be a man."

"I wouldn't mind that. As long as my boy is safe. And not hearing weird noises echoing in the house would surely be a blessing."

"You can give him the pass for his birthday," said Carlos. "Just don't let him know it came from you or me. We can tell him it's from Irving."

"Perfect," said Lara. "I'm sure Irv will make it back for José's birthday to present the gift."

Carlos added, "Don't forget, we have family working on dairy farms up north. They would be happy to take him in and teach him how to milk cows. Farm work will teach him lessons he can't get anywhere else."

"I'm sure José would be up for that," said Lara "He likes animals, and it's got to be better than playing with noisy toys in the basement."

"I'll let them know he's coming."

"That sounds wonderful," said Lara. "I'm sure he can make some new friends. Or any friends. That would be nice, too."

Chapter 07 -
Time for a Spam™ Burrito

The conversation stopped as José came up the stairs.

Having the adults in the room stop talking as you enter is never a good sign, but José didn't notice. He had so many other things on his mind, the first and foremost being food

"I made some breakfast burritos, with Spam™ and boiled potatoes," Lara said.

"My favorite!"

"And your uncle brought some hot sauce from New York City. The ads on TV say it's the best."

José nodded, ready to try the famous hot sauce.

"I hope it's not too hot," said Lara. "My boy has a sensitive stomach."

"Don't worry," said Carlos. "It's from New York. What do they know about real hot sauce? Don't believe everything you see on TV."

Lara dabbed a bit of the sauce on José's plate, then looked over to her brother-in-law for assurance.

José dug into the tasty treat, cutting off the chance for questions for a few minutes, until the dam broke.

"Are you going to tell us where you went so early in the morning?" asked Lara.

"I told you yesterday, *Madre*," said José. "I was up early to test my TimeMachine."

"My book club friends called me this morning. They said you were heading up to the foothills. There was hardly any light. You could have been run over."

"I was careful."

Carlos stepped in to help Lara and defend his *sobrino* from accusations, neighbors, and imagined monsters.

"Your mother is right," said Carlos. "It's dangerous riding a bike at night, and the road up the ridge line is narrow. You do know that time machines are only fantasy, right? We don't live inside an H.G. Wells story. It was just a book."

"And a radio and a TV show," said José . "But that isn't the point. I'm telling the truth, I was testing out a TimeWall breaking machine."

Tio Carlos shook his head. "That's fine, José. We don't really need to know, as long as you weren't doing anything illegal. Or drugs."

This is a waste of time. Even my tio doesn't understand what I'm doing.

"Drugs? Why would I do that?" said José. "I have way more interesting things to do than ingest weird chemicals."

Carlos raised an eyebrow and smiled.

There wasn't much need for more conversation at the breakfast table. Fresh Spam™ and potato burritos were more important than discussions, especially when the only topic would be what he was doing so early in the morning wandering about in the damp grass.

"Thanks for the breakfast *Madre*," said José. "I've got things to do in my workshop."

"Take Paquito with you," said Lara. "He'll protect you from any monsters you might run into.'

José shook his head and said, "Com'on Paquito. Let's go find those monsters. I've got some treats on my worktable."

He closed the door behind him as he and Paquito left the warmth of the kitchen for his cold basement hideaway.

Carlos sipped his coffee and said, "Don't worry Lara, his experiments will fail and he'll soon take up another interest. The boy's got a lot of energy, and on the plus side, he's learning about electronics."

"He could go to a trade school," said Lara. "It'll be safer and he could make friends with the other students. I don't like him down in that basement, fiddling with tools. The boy needs some direction. His father should be here to give it to him."

Carlos took that as his invitation to leave, before the discussion turned to his wandering brother and his fate. "I have to go back to the university. I'll come by again and check on the boy tonight, if that's okay with you?"

"*Gracias*. You're welcome to join us for dinner," said Lara.

In the basement, José talked to his tiny assistant as he looked over his backpack, the smell of overheated capacitors saturating the air. "I'll extract the data to the computer's drive first. I don't want to risk a hardware failure."

He plugged in a 5MB drive he scavenged from a discarded computer he picked up from the High School trash bin, then daisy-chained a few more.

"20 megabytes should be more than enough," he said to Paquito over the din of spinning platters.

The noise of computer platters and their failing bearings couldn't be ignored.

"I bet I could use this sound all by itself to open a hole in the TimeWall. It's sure loud, it wouldn't take much to boost it. I might be able to generate sounds and record at the same time."

The drives were barely up to speed and strange clacking sounds were making their status known.

"I better shut this down, I don't trust those platters, they could explode and destroy all my data," said José. "I don't want my *madre* to start bugging me again about the noise. I can check the video, that should be quieter. Later, I'll look around for some different hard drives, something with some life left in it."

José connected the RCA jacks to the monitor and hit play. The video didn't help. It looked like the blast from the cracked TimeWall knocked over the recorder, it only played wild wailing and a view of fog and grass as it hit the ground.

"That's disappointing. Maybe the sensors have some data I can extract. I can always move the data to permanent storage after I replace the hard drives."

He had a state-of-the-art Atari CX40 his *tio* gave him for his birthday and he used it to view the data from the simple sensors of the day.

My mother should be proud, thought José. *She used to worry that I would become caught up in the video games. I'm sure that some of her friends even claimed the games were controlled by the devil.* Luckily for José and his mother, Diablo never made its presence known and the games were quietly ignored.

A few tweaks of the game controllers sucked the data to the toy's internal storage and broadcast it to the Atari-supplied monitor. Every sensor report was a fuzzy gray fog.

"It's all noise. I've got nothing here. No one will believe me without hard evidence."

He sat, head in hand trying to make sense of the information. "I bet the sensor array got wiped passing back through the TimeWall. I should have checked the recordings before I returned."

The boy scientist, optimistic as always, took every failure as an opportunity, trying to reason out a solution. He was not willing to be denied so easily.

"I know what. I need to do it again with better cameras and a wider sensor range or maybe wrap everything in tinfoil before exiting. Better yet. Old school, I'll go full analog. I just have to find my Polaroid camera and buy some fresh film. ISO 400 should work. No worries, I have time on my side."

Chapter 08-
Time for Some Noise

The crickets kept count and José calculated the outside air temperature while the quiet banshees' singing lulled him to sleep. His mind kept active, reviewing all he had witnessed in his short interaction with the TimeWall. He woke up early, still worried about his dreams but determined to continue his experiment. He snuck down to the kitchen and noticed his *tio's* sports car parked out front. *I better be quiet. I guess Tio stayed in the spare bedroom. I'll grab a bowl of cornflakes and go down to the basement,* thought José.

It took a few days to find and replace the failed equipment before he could return to his special testing area, but when everything was ready, José packed up his bike and left at the crack of dawn. His mother liked to sleep in on weekends and his *tio* was at the university working on his dissertation. José still couldn't drive and it was a long haul up to the staging area on his bicycle.

José looked up and down the trail leading from the nearby town. "There's no one on the path, so this is as good a time as any to try again."

He reached for the controls on his backpack, adjusting rheostats for frequency and volume.

"I think it needs more volume and maybe an increase in the oscillation frequency to keep the wall in place longer. I can't forget to turn on the video recorder. I hope I don't run out of tape."

The TimeWall had passed, but Time was pervasive, ethereal, and still part of his existence. Time trembled and bubbled as quantum banshees beat against the tenuous structure defining the wall.

If only I could snap a picture beyond the wall, he thought, *then this experiment would be a success.*

José staggered as angry fourth-dimensional bubbles making up the TimeWall pushed at the interloper, each time-packet unique. The average indicates a solid wall, the summation of discrete blobs, becoming the Now. It was a differential dancing wall of quantum pellets tearing its way forward in the one-way flow we call Time.

He was ready for the onslaught this time around and could handle the twisting bubbles tearing at his guts and neurons as he pushed the leading sensor arrays through the wall. His headset displayed gray echoes of his last reality on the small screen.

Do I push forward through the wall or wait for it to pass, leaving me beyond the barrier? Time focused on the unwelcome intruder and José stepped back as the bombardment of time bubbles pushed at the Now and the tiny human in their way.

But José was no quitter. He pushed back at the nebulous wall, ripping his goggles off to get a clear view, eyesight be damned. A gray, almost human shape with a flat face and glasses confronted him. He heard echoes of sound in a voice almost identical to his.

Time travel was nothing like the TV tropes; there was no way to go back and change history. As soon as he crossed the time line he was faced with his past; a virtual unending sequence of time slices, a slinky linked by QTmBits representing all he knew and how he lived. Once behind the TimeWall, it was gray and foggy, smelling of rot and mold, but it was his to explore where no one had been before.

A dark flat face, resembling José, demanded an answer.

>What are you doing here? You're not allowed on this side of Time.

A string of likenesses approached, murmuring, complaining, threatening.

"Who are you?" shouted José. "Are you me? Get away from me!"

Words did nothing to slow down the approaching horde.

>Toss him back.

>>Push our host beyond Time. He doesn't belong here.

>Force him to the ground.

>>>Kick him back to the Now, now.

The angry group approached, thin shadows of himself, swarming over José

The mass of gray Shadows attacking José filled his head with old memories, pushing him back against the moving TimeWall.

"I see what you're doing!" José shouted. "You're me, my Shadows. My memories, my history, and you're trying to chase me away."

José thrashed around, waving his hands to disperse the onslaught of molecular-thin representations. His Shadows smothered his Now and filled his head with thoughts he may have wanted to keep repressed. His wild flaying cleared a space, knocking his Shadows around like attacking bees.

He was pushed back against the moving TimeWall. Time bubbles surrounded his world, bursting explosions twisted in his brain, painting pictures behind his eyes. He would have had a better look at the surroundings, but his glasses froze up in the icy grip of past-time.

Was it an instant or an infinity? José felt trapped in the swirling existence of unknown dimensions. The wall fought back with all its skill, or nothing at all. It was hard to tell.

Time bubbles focused on his backpack, shorting capacitors, blowing out vacuum tubes, interrupting quantum interactions, wreaking havoc at his shoulders. Dying bubbles began imitating his sound generators, loud angry banshee wails dominating his surroundings, harmonizing in frequencies and patterns unknown to the outside world.

José struggled to his feet and faced his past. The Shadow at the front of the line shook its head, stepped up to José, and gave him a shove. Time bubbles exploded, screaming back at José and his backpack as the TimeWall opening weakens and shatters. He fell back into the wet grass and mud. His last clear thought was of the Shadows swarming over, attacking with an unyielding string of memories.

He lay in the clearing, his line of Shadows lost to the past, the TimeWall slowly dissipating, bubbles bursting and melting in the onslaught of the Now. Time didn't notice the kerfuffle and steadily moved away, waiting patiently, hardly aware of the actions in its immediate past.

"That was weird," said José. "I better be careful. My Shadows don't seem to be very friendly. Maybe I can convince them of my good intentions. I wonder if they like candy."

José shook his head, trying to make sense of what he just experienced.

"This is not what I was expecting. I don't want to re-live my life right now and I'm not ready to be dead yet."

José lay in the grass, the foothills and sky ignoring the tiny figure. He was in a fugue state, reliving bits and pieces of his past in excruciating detail.

Be that as it may, Time passed, and José was alone in an open field, bathed in the Now, with a backpack filled with broken, smoking electronic waste.

José felt failure and elation. He failed to step behind Time's wall for more than a moment but at least he could make it appear at will with his quantum diddling.

José hoisted his backpack, still smoking from the attacks of the time bubbles and trekked back to where his bike was stashed.

"I better secure the gear; it's a long trip back and downhill most of the way. Good thing I replaced the brake pads."

He could have called his mother for a ride, but he didn't want to deal with the inevitable third-degree about why he was so far from home at the crack of dawn. Explaining his theories was out of the question, and wandering around the distant hills couldn't be justified in any normal discussion. It seemed that any discourse with his mother ended up with a plea to settle down and deliver grandchildren. It wasn't that he disliked other people, but except for his immediate family, he had no need for any other human in his life at the moment.

He was excited to check the data flow and learn a little more about the TimeWall. He had weeks to analyze the information as he rebuilt his equipment and attempted another run at the TimeWall.

I'm sure there's some valid data buried beneath the gray noise, thought José. *I just have to twiddle the bits and pull it out from the blocking background.* Despite his assurances, there was nothing but gray static, filling up every data point.

Chapter 09-
Time Baby

José spent the better part of the afternoon and into the night working on his recordings. He was disappointed that, despite his best efforts, they were all for naught. Without some reproducible records, it was his word against Time's. Not that Time would speak up for itself, since it was incommunicado for all intents and purposes.

Carlos was upstairs spending some more time with his mother. José shrugged at the situation and said goodnight to both as they sat drinking coffee at the kitchen table. It wasn't unusual for his mother and Carlos to stay up late discussing the events of the day, and probably planning his future in detail. Not that he cared. They could talk about anything they wanted; it wouldn't affect his experiments.

It was night, with nothing but the sound of crickets to bother the insomniacs and lull the sleeping households. José heard every chirp and scratch of the insects' legs. But instead of an annoying noise, José heard distinct voices. He thought that he could name each cricket in his neighborhood. He concentrated on checking the air temperature from his friends, trying to hide the nightmare of his Shadows, pushing him out of Time.

Gray faces flipped in his mind, each one a slice of his past. Ancient, half-remembered memories continued to flood his head. He saw himself in his bassinet, wet and crying. Two blobs stood over the crib, saying soothing words to the young José.

This can't be real, thought José. *You're not supposed to remember early life. I'm sure I was too young to keep that type of memory. This better not take me back to the womb.*

He surrendered to the grays, letting the vignettes play out in his mind. *This is no worse than counting sheep,* thought José. *I'll be asleep soon and away from these bad dreams.*

Everything was a blur, not just from undeveloped eyes but serious astigmatism, a gift from his genes, activated at birth. In his mind, he recognized the clock on the bureau, a classic flip; white numbers on a black background. Between eating and excreting, boredom took over, and he learned the pattern without knowing the meanings. Each minute clicked, echoes dropping off as seconds were softly counted in the 60-cycle electric buzz flying through the house wiring.

Did the butterfly-like wings of the turning clock lead to his time experiments? Each flip twisted the air, electric hums becoming whispers of soft wails that only he could hear.

José thought, *Was his experiences just light reflecting off the mobile over his crib and noisy power lines?*

He shook his head, dislodging the ancient doubts forcing themselves into his consciousness.

Even if my TimeWall experiments were based on misunderstood random lights and sounds, how could the TimeWall appearance the other day not be true?

There was nothing new to learn from baby José. Being a baby was pretty much a full-time job and with no reference point, he took life as it was presented.

Baby José flipped out of sight and mind. Another gray face, older, but almost the same as the previous one, became his muse. His hearing was acute, eyesight, not so much. He was re-living himself as a toddler, walking around and bouncing off corners he could barely see. No matter where he went, he could hear the banshee songs, calling him, trying to get his attention. He mostly ignored the siren call of the singers, and after a while it became the background sound of his life. Baby tinnitus, noise, and nothing more.

For José, the playbacks were his memories. His TimeSlices contained every moment of his life and the Shadows spun the records back as if he was living them in real time. Cross connections behind the TimeWall expanded the scope of the memories.

In the master bedroom, his parents discussed their son, hoping to set him on the right path.

Lara said, "Irv, I think we have to get that boy checked. He's starting to show bruises from bumping into things."

"He's fine," said Irving. "It's normal for a few bumps and bruises in little kids. He'll grow out of it."

"I'm afraid we'll get called in by the police. They'll think we're abusing our child."

"That's ridiculous. Look how healthy he is."

"He looks skinny and frail."

"Just feed him more. How about some Spam™ burritos? He loves those."

"Well, you like them," said Lara. "The poor child hardly has any teeth yet."

José didn't remember this interaction as it played back in his head, but it was his reality and he did like Spam™ burritos. His gray friends took control of his timeline and moved beyond dirty diapers.

More flips, more dreams. José struggled to keep his thoughts and his Shadows in control. Elementary school sped by. There was nothing to see until first grade, where he got a pair of glasses. The world came into focus, and he strode around seeing everything in a new light. The banshees slipped quietly away into the background, ready to bother some other poor soul with their constant wailing.

José discovered reading and was soon inhaling every written word he could get his hands on. Cereal boxes, candy wrappers, newspapers and even books. He rapidly expanded his vocabulary, sneaking books from the library after having his card threatened for taking out too many books at once.

His gray Shadows must have been having fun as they found some intersection nodes and played back the library interactions for José's edification.

"Look, Hazel, here comes that strange kid again," said Francisca, the librarian.

"What's he doing?" said Hazel. "He just checked out those three books this morning. Does he have mental issues? Can he even understand what's in the books?"

"I know," said Francisca. "A middle school kid can't read that fast. I checked and most of the books are science fiction. I swear he's read almost every book in that genre we have on the shelves."

"He sure is skinny for a kid. Are you sure he's that old?" said Hazel. "Aren't some of the sci-fi topics a little racy for a child? I think we should put most of them in a restricted adult section."

"I don't know," said Francisca. "I've never read science fiction; I prefer history books."

"And romance," said Hazel under her breath.

"I know what to do," said Francisca. "Let's ask him about the books. If he's actually reading, he'll be able to give us a book report of sorts."

"Perfect. You can do it," said Hazel. "You're almost a child yourself."

"Sure," said Francisca quietly, "Your blue hair would probably scare the poor kid."

Gray-memory played back the interactions perfectly. José didn't remember the words at the moment, but they were accessible as recorded time-slices from his growing brain and Shadow connections.

José recalled looking at his feet and mumbling something, something about something and in return received a temporary restriction on his precious library card. He was limited to one book a day and had to give a summary before he would be able to check out another book.

In response to the snub and forced book reports, José took an alternative path from the hall of books and knowledge. After school he went to the mall and began a deep dive into comic books. They were fun and light reading, but couldn't hold a candle to the pictures he could draw in his mind while reading the popular sci-fi books of the period.

He flipped through the comic books at full speed, reading the text and barely glancing at the pictures. He only stopped when the book clerks insisted he buy the books rather than sit there and read. Something about not being a lending library and wanting their 25¢ for each book.

Fortunately, Hazel retired and speed-reading became a thing. A slightly older José returned to his source of knowledge and began mainlining books again, without interference.

His gray Shadows glossed over the enjoyment he got from the books. José would have preferred to linger and revisit the sci-fi worlds he loved. On the plus side, he could always go back and re-read anything he wanted, anytime he wanted.

Chapter 10 -
Time for a Burrito

José's family home was a typical two-story suburban domicile. His bedroom was upstairs facing a small backyard. His mother had the master bedroom and his father, when he was in town, was often relegated to the guest room.

The house was old, even before his parents became sole owners. It was built on rock quarried locally and stood strong with its original thick stone walls. In the winter, the rocks became the same temperature as the ice clinging to them. Every freeze and melt loosened the mortar, making the structure a little weaker and exposed for the next cycle.

No normal sounds could pass through the walls. If you listened carefully, you could hear the rocks sing their song of existence and experiences, but it was at a frequency and duration unknown to most humans.

In summer, the basement was a haven from the hot, humid air. It was practically the only place to work in the house until air conditioning isolated them from the world. Sheet rock and insulation stabilized the house at whatever price they could afford to blow through the system.

José used the basement as his private enclave, a place to quietly study anything that caught his fancy. His work area grew organically as he followed one interest to another. No matter if it was identifying insects, mushrooms, or listening for Time's quiet echo. Each experience was neatly packed, labeled, and tucked away in case the interest carousel rolled back into view.

When family times were happier, his *tio*, the professor, and his current wife, the blond bimbo, would join the family for weekend barbecues. Seared meat, cooked with hot peppers, onion, citrus, and spices was their usual barbecue entrée. On special days there were hot potato pancakes, fried to a golden brown. After a couple of beers into the night, his *tio* would start expounding on Time theories and historical stories of ghosts, *La Llorona*, and *Chupacabra*.

"José," asked Carlos. "What do you know about Time?"

"I don't want to hear about your *meshuggeneh* theories," said Lara. "The boy is barely able to wake up for school on time. If you get him confused about what time it is, he'll never graduate."

"Just one little theory, to whet his interest. The more he knows, the safer he'll be."

"Safer from what?"

"Things that go bump in the night, of course," said Carlos.

"That's not what you need to discuss. Quit talking about monsters," said Lara. "Next you're going to tell us there's a golem in your time fantasies. Is Diablo himself leading you down this path? Do I need to call a priest?"

"Or a rabbi?" said Carlos suggested with a grin.

Lara gave her brother-in-law a dirty look.

José sat at the picnic table, playing with his food, as the discourse bounced back and forth. He knew better than to interrupt the discussions when his mother had the floor.

"Sorry," said Carlos. "I'm only trying to give the kid some options. How can it hurt? It's not good to lead such a sheltered life. The boy needs to expand his horizons."

"Stop playing with your burrito," admonished his mother. "I made it special, with those habanero chiles you like." Without missing a beat she turned to Carlos, "You know the boy is sensitive, *le estas llenando la cabeza de tontería.*"

"It's not nonsense. There's some scientific basis for those theories," said Carlos.

José bit into his burrito, hot sauce spilling out the bottom. He didn't say anything; the adults held the floor and he had enough sense to keep out of the way of dangerous verbal barbs.

"He's smart enough to know that monsters don't exist," said Carlos. He turned to José, "You don't believe in monsters? Do you?"

José wasn't sure if this question was a trap, but answered as best he could. "I don't know about the monsters you mentioned. They don't scare me, all they can do is shake the bed late at night."

"See!" Lara said. "He's already taking your hair-brained theories and getting upset. His father should be here to set him straight."

Carlos took a long sip of his beer and asked José, "Did you see the game last night? It was quite a show."

41

José wanted to agree, but he didn't know which sport his *tio* was talking about. It was summer, so baseball was his best bet. "Yes, *Tio*. I really enjoyed watching the batters and runners."

Carlos said, "See? He's fine, Lara, he follows sports like every other kid. Tell you what, I'll take him to a ball game next week."

"You don't have to do that," said Lara. "His father will be back soon and he can take the boy."

"Even better, we can all go. Irving, José, and I will go to the ballpark next week. How does that sound, José?"

"That's fine, *Tio*," said José. "Can I get a hot dog?"

"Of course. I'll pick up you and your dad and we'll make a day of it."

José wasn't concerned. His father rarely made it back home on a regular schedule and seemed to make it a habit to ignore whatever his son was interested in. José didn't know what his father did for a living and no one ever discussed it. As long as he had his *madre,* his workshop, and his candy-apple red bike, he was fine.

José pushed his chair back and left his family to continue discussing the world, food, and beer. No one noticed his absence.

His immediate family left him to his own devices in the basement, and even his favorite uncle seldom entered José's sanctuary. It didn't start off as a laboratory; originally it was a place to store junk before later transforming into a small shop used to tinker with his bike. It would take years to shape the room into its life's work. For now the basement didn't know anything about its future position in the world and accepted whatever was dropped into it.

José opened the side door leading to the basement. It didn't creak like a horror movie; his OCD-enhanced mechanical skills ensured that WD-40™ was always at the ready. Boxes, books, and tools were stacked, each in its place, ready to be activated whenever José's interest shifted. It wasn't hoarding so much as storage for the collective detritus of familial living.

Chapter 11-
Time for High School

Before his first experience with the TimeWall, he had to deal with high school and all the permutations of rooms full of rowdy, rude compatriots. José didn't fit into any standard box, and his overriding intelligence frightened not only most of the students but some of the staff as well.

His mixture of Mexican and Jewish heritage, a 'Jewican' as his peers sometimes referred to it, did not bode well in any modern American high school, and making friends was not part of his regular skill set.

The science nerds tended to stick together, not necessarily for company but for security. His only friend was Hector, his neighbor. Hector was taller than José, with sandy-blonde hair and thin. Hector would occasionally step in to help his friend when the jocks, bullies and cool kids began to bother the smaller nerds. He didn't go overboard. The risk of losing what little cool he possessed was more important than defending every slight José had to deal with.

The reports from his school counselor noted José's uncompromising attention to detail and bulldog determination. The counselors discussed their charges over coffee and donuts in the faculty lounge, trying to make sense of the atypical kids.

"So, how many independent study kids do we have this year?" asked the assistant principal.

"You should know. You assigned them to us. But to answer your question, it's seven so far. It's getting worse and worse every year," said the Algebra instructor.

"I blame the movies. All this outer space sci-fi stuff is warping their minds. It was so much better in my day when we had to read and use our own imagination."

"They all think they're Vulcan-brained scientists, whatever that means."

"Or worse, the ones who try to speak made-up movie language. Who could even understand what they're saying?"

"At least most of the special students gravitate to theater. Those classes let them act out their fantastical delusions."

"And keep them out of my class," said the algebra teacher.

Nervous laughter filled the break room. Everyone was afraid of being assigned one of the weird kids. It wasn't that they drooled over the linoleum floors, although that wasn't an unusual trait. It was the never-ending questions and search for answers that bothered most of the teachers.

"That one curly head kid, Juan or something like that, is a real number. He won't socialize with the other students and is always tinkering with some electric doodad or another."

"I don't see that as being bad, except for Jonese over here, who has to deal with him in the electronics classes."

"That's right," said Jonese. "I caught him sneaking out some old vacuum tubes we had in the back. Not that I have any use for ancient technology, but what else is he planning on doing with obsolete equipment?"

"Nothing explosive, I hope."

The biology teacher put down the copy of Teachers Weekly he was hiding behind and said, "Look, they have a whole article here about dealing with uncontrollable students. It's a little pill called 'Ritalin'."

"Does it work?"

"That's what the article says. Maybe we should get some and give it a try?"

"I know just the student I'd like to try it on," said Jonese.

"In the meantime, let's put Juan or Joe or whatever his name is in with the independent study group. Who wants to be his main contact?"

No one raised a hand, and more than one headed for the door, before the bell rang.

"How about you, Jonese?" asked the assistant principal. "He seems to like electronics and woodworking. He'll fit in perfectly."

"And maybe even teach you a thing or two," whispered one of the English teachers.

44

It was almost unanimous and they decided it would be best to toss him in the creative arts bucket or let him become part of the drug abusers. It wasn't a great career move, but it kept him away from their classrooms and lessened the chance of confusing the education process by asking questions they didn't understand. Fortunately for José, his school was reasonably progressive and had a policy of not yet overmedicating their charges to meet a definition of 'normal' unless they were completely off the rails.

Abandoning the unusual kids to their own devices was considered the best way for them to fit into the curriculum. After all, what would a group of regular, underpaid, over-educated teachers do once the weird kids started banging on their doors? They stashed José in with the other outliers, hoping that interacting with something like his own kind would drag him along an educational path and out the door in a few years.

Being part of the special study group left him on his own to explore multiple avenues of interest. He had access to electronics, woodworking, metal-smithing, and the science labs when they weren't in use. Unlike his peers, he didn't spend unallocated time smoking cheap marijuana outside the school's hallowed halls. He used his poor communication skills to his advantage, telling few about his interests and proclivities. Those with whom he discussed his TimeWall theories chalked it up to the effect of high-school quality drugs, assuming José was on the same plane as they were. Of course, discussions were immediately forgotten, in a drug-twisted haze.

No chess trophies for our young charge. He could easily win most games, but he felt uncomfortable being in the spotlight. Feigning incompetence was the easy way out. A combination of seasonal flu and nausea ended any chance of José earning a black-belt in chess. Sports were equally out of the question. Why risk getting beat up in even more venues? He was happy to follow a different path, letting his inclinations lead him along.

José's life during his high school years wasn't all hard work and focused introspection. He had a habit of watching bad movies and TV shows whose plots revolved around TimeTravelers.

José enjoyed the fictional Time episodes even if they didn't fit his concepts. He thought that if someone could travel back in time it would cause ripples in history that would affect the active Now. He never saw his world changing from the effects of a Time ripple.

The possibilities the screenwriters for TV and movies had developed never made sense to him, it seemed to require multiple static pieces of existence, stuck in the same time segment. Till what? Do they merge in the future or do they extend, running in their own space, until the end of Time?

Those theories didn't jive with José's concept of Time. Maybe the soft banshee singing almost every night instructed him on the vagaries of Time. He was sure that there was not a place in Time you could step into and continue to exist while interacting in that space going forward.

José didn't know what the fullness of Time was hiding, but he figured he would work on a single feature to increase the chances of success.

If Time has a direction, then it's moving, *ipso facto,* there must be a front that may be accessible.

By that fact alone, he doubted his high school peers understood what his theories meant.

Chapter 12 -
Time for Star Trek®

José was alone in the electronic lab working on his TimeWall designs. His usual accomplice, Hector, was nowhere to be found. The bell rang and students filed in, ready to struggle through another fifty minutes of an incomprehensible lecture and overly safe experiments.

The administrators had long decided to keep the risk of lawsuits to a minimum. The students were limited to low-power electrical experiments with the hope that some would understand basic concepts without getting a serious shock.

José glanced at the lesson plan on his way out. The students would have to build a breadboard and populate it with a dual-pole, double-throw knife switch connected to a battery and bulb. José shook his head in disbelief seeing the low-risk experiment the students were allowed.

I wonder how many of the students can build something that complex, let alone understand how electrons flow, thought José.

"That reminds me," said to himself, "I wonder if my *madre* would be willing to ask the electric company to drop in another 100amp line. I'm sure they would be happy to sell more power."

José quickly tossed his partially completed breadboard into his backpack and left for the next class on his roster: 'Independent Studies'. It was a nice bonus for the smart kids and it kept them from disturbing the teachers and students with difficult questions.

"I hope no one messes with my equipment. I'm sure I tucked the capacitors safely away. I wouldn't want them to get hurt."

He wandered down the hallway, peeking into each room, looking for lab space with no students sitting around listening to boring lectures.

Well, this is inconvenient, he thought. *All the places I'd like to go are filled with students, and I don't want to deal with that. What am I going to do for the next class period?*

47

The cafeteria was closed and even with an hour of self-instruction, wandering around with nothing to do was frowned upon by the teachers. There were one too many times over the years that some random free-spirited student would peek through the narrow door window and disrupt a class with funny faces.

The only option was to join the creative/outcast kids behind the tennis courts, where they discussed the fantasies of the day.

I hope they aren't smoking those weird cigarettes. It always seems to give me a headache, thought José

The usual crowd was hanging out between class periods. Theater kids, a football jock, his girlfriend, and a few dedicated stoners who were always welcome wherever drugs were an option. His neighbor, Hector, was leaning against a post, wasting time between classes.

"Hey look," said one of the long-haired semi-students. "Here comes the nerd."

"Don't be mean," said the hulking football kid. "He helped me with my math test."

"Oh, right. You were about to be kicked off the team. What did you get? A 'D+'?"

"No. It was a 'C-minus, thank you very much'. The best grade I've ever earned."

"How'd that work? Did the nerd sneak in and take the test for you? He doesn't look much like a football player."

"Hey. I earned that grade all by myself," said the football kid. "With only a little help from José."

The girl standing behind her huge boyfriend whispered, "I don't care, he gives me the creeps!"

José walked up as one of the students fired up a hand-rolled cigarette. He nodded to Hector, both of them on the outskirts of the group.

"I found my brother's stash. I overheard his dealer say it was real good ganja."

"Are you sure? Is it really from Jamaica? It looks more like stems and seeds," said stoner number two.

"Of course I'm sure. If you can't trust a dealer, who can you trust? Do you want a hit or not?"

The tennis court filled with the smell of cheap weed as the miscreants became more intoxicated. It was a psychological high for the most part since the leftover shake these kids were smoking had more toxic smoke than THC.

As with any meeting of the minds, they had a theme: the latest Star Trek® movie, 'The Voyage Home'.

"Can you believe they went back in time?" said stoner number one. "Just think, future us could be here right now."

Stoner number two looked around and saw nothing. He replied as only a stoner could. "Yeah, man."

"Sure, like you're going to be part of a starship," said the football jock's girlfriend. "You'll be lucky to afford a bus ticket."

"Okay, so maybe not us, but others might be here, watching our every move."

"Like aliens?"

"No, dumbass. There was only one alien in the show, Mr. Spock."

"He was the smart one, right?"

The girlfriend peeked out at José and said, "He looks like a Spock."

"Hey, four-eyes, let's see what's behind those curly locks. Are there pointed ears?"

"I bet his tan is fake. Does he have green skin?"

"You want a toke, José?" asked stoner number two.

"Don't do that," said the jock. "He'll drone on and on about time barriers and science nonsense."

"Hey guys," said José. "I overheard you talking about the star-whale movie. Did you know that the way they did the time travel scene was incorrect?"

The girlfriend sighed.

"No, really," said José. "You can't just go fast and go back in time. That was a myth from the Superman comics."

"So now he's a comic expert, too?" said stoner number one in a distinct *sotto voce*.

"I am," said José. "The writers needed a way for Superman to go back and they imagined that time was behind us, so moving fast counterclockwise will get you there."

"I suppose you know better," sneered one of the hangers-on. "Have you tried it? Can you travel to the past?"

"Or better yet, the future? Can you take a look at next week's final exams? Now that would be a worthwhile trip."

Snickering by the stoners emphasized the questions.

"Well, not exactly, but I have a few theories I'm testing out," said José.

"See? I knew he was a Spock," said the girlfriend.

"A Vulcan," said a stoner. "Spock was his name, his race was Vulcan."

"Whatever," said the girlfriend.

"We don't need to learn about your theories. We're on a different path of enlightenment."

"Yeah. One with drugs," said stoner number two.

Jose looked around the empty tennis courts, with their sagging, ripped net, and said nothing.

If this is the path to enlightenment, thought José. *I think they're stuck in the slow lane.*

Hector held back, "Just a few more months and I can graduate. I'm joining the Marines. You should join up, too."

"Thanks for the offer," said José. "But I am determined to go to college. Maybe later."

The classroom bell rang. José looked at his schedule. It still said Independent Study, but it was in the electronics lab. Empty. Just the way he liked it.

The other students scurried off to their next interaction with education, while the potheads slunk into the background, waiting for the next set of kids ready to learn by doing drugs.

Chapter 13 -
Time to Borrow the Car

High school shop classes were great fun, but inadequate for José's ambitious projects. Despite limited resources and restrictions on when he could work on his experiments, he was able to hone his skills on the school's dime. He used his experience to set up a small workshop in his basement. The thick rock walls proved ideal in muffling the sounds of his devices and shielding his work from nosy neighbors.

Even so, as his experiments became more complex, loud noises radiated beyond the basement walls and, over time, the research did begin to disturb the neighbors. It was summer and he had months to work on his ideas until he would be forced to join his peers in buildings filled with unending boredom and the general abuse called 'high school'.

Whether his immediate family thought he was learning a weird instrument or enjoyed Tibetan throat singing, they never said. In his case, the lack of girlfriends joining his basement studies probably kept him out of prison or at least ensured he was not a suspect in any teenage vandalism cropping up throughout the neighborhood.

Above the surreal world of José's basement experiments, his mother and uncle discussed his situation over a cup of coffee.

"He started up with that noise again," said Lara. "That boy is going to be the death of me. I hope the police don't visit again. How would I explain what he is doing?"

"It's just growing pains," said Carlos. "I think he needs to get out and see the world. Maybe it's time to make use of the bus pass? A few months on the road will do him good."

"He's too young and skinny," said Lara. "And if you think I'm going to travel cross-country with that boy, you have another think coming."

"Now, Lara, it's good to expand horizons. José can take care of himself. We're all tough *hombres* on our side of the family."

"I suppose so. And it would be good to get him out of the house for a while."

"Exactly. I have friends at some of the colleges nearby. He can visit them, do some exploring. It will be good for him."

Lara said, "Good. Maybe he'll forget about his weird experiments. Do you think I can sell the junk in the basement when he's on the road?"

"No. You should wait on that until he gets back. It's better if he sells off his toys on his own volition. There could be repercussions if you remove his equipment without his permission. His life is tied to the equipment and it could be bad if it suddenly disappeared. Then he might double down and buy more. You must allow him to move at his own pace."

"Okay. It's probably better that way. He can be very stubborn. I don't even clean the basement anymore. I don't want to go through that again."

In spite of his *tio*'s encouragement to leave at once and explore the world outside his basement laboratory, José wanted to test his latest iteration of his experiments one more time.

He stuck his head out the basement door and shouted, "Mom, I'm going out. Can I borrow the car?"

"Are you going to meet your friends?"

"I'm going to test some new equipment."

There was disappointment in his mother's voice as she tried another tact to get her son on a normal path.

"There's a new Star Space movie my book club told me about. Their kids seem to like it a lot. You should go with your friends, maybe take a date."

"You mean Star Trek? I've already seen that movie."

"Your *tio* said he would pay for pizza for your date."

Carlos looked up from his coffee and shook his head 'No.'

"Thanks, *madre*, but I'm not going on a date to please my *tio*. I have other plans."

"You're not going to take your noise-makers out in public, are you? I've been getting calls from the neighbors."

"Don't worry. I'll keep well away from your nosy coffee klatch friends."

"Don't insult my book club! We're all that's keeping this neighborhood together. Who knows what evil *fantasma* could sneak in if we weren't watching out."

José wanted to explain that ghosts weren't real, but took the path of least resistance and didn't reply. The sooner the tirade was over the sooner he could get back to his experiments. He could have mentioned the fact that he had looked and there were no ghosts behind the time wall, but that would bring up more questions he preferred to avoid. The gentle suggestions from his *madre* continued, not nagging, but something quite like it.

"Maybe you should go see a nice, calming movie. The Star ones have too much violence, I've heard."

"Yes. I'll do that."

Another suggestion shot down, but his mother pulled out her ace in the hole.

"Are you going to use the bus pass your father gifted you? He would be insulted if you stayed in the basement all summer. You should get out while the weather is nice. I can give you the addresses of some of your cousins. I think they have jobs on farms up North."

"I plan to travel once I test out a few things. And I am not going to work on a farm, no matter how much fun that would be. In fact, I'm looking forward to the bus trip. It would be a great opportunity to find equipment for my devices. You wouldn't believe it, but vacuum tubes are hard to find in this town."

"Before I forget," said his mother. "Your *tio* has contacts at some of the colleges. He told me he can introduce you to the professors. Maybe you'll find a nice college that you like after high school."

"Okay."

"In the meantime, I promised your cousins you would visit. Farm work would do you good. You might want to become a vet or learn to drive a tractor."

"I'll consider it, although I'll tell you right now, farm work is not for me."

"Are you taking an attitude with me José Isaac Davidovich? You know I don't like that."

"It's just a statement of fact. I'm going to borrow your car if you don't need it."

53

"If you must. Just don't be late, your *tio* has some things he wants to give you for the trip. He'll be coming over before you leave. You are going, aren't you? He took a risk arranging for the bus pass and I expect that you won't want to disappoint him."

You mean the one Papa gave me?"

"Yes… I mis-spoke."

"Sure," said José. "I have to get my gear ready."

José turned to go back to the basement, ready for the solitude of the open hills and the noise of his banshee-blasting sound system.

He didn't get far.

His mother worked on the principle that repeating a question made it more likely the recipient would do as she wanted, as she circled back to the request of the moment.

"Please don't use your noise-maker. My friends are starting to complain."

"Don't worry, *madre*. I'll take it out of town first thing in the morning, so no one will be disturbed by the sounds."

"I don't see why you have to make so much noise. It's as bad as if you were playing the bagpipes."

"We're not Scottish. I'll be back before you know it. I've got lots of time."

"Are you going to be out late? Do you want a sandwich? I bought the cookies you like."

"That'll be fine, madre. I'll be back before dinner."

"You'll need breakfast. I can make some burritos in the morning before you leave if you want."

"No need. I'll be up early and I'll try not to disturb you or the neighbors."

Chapter 14 -
Time for Another

The soft wailing wouldn't stop.

José knew empirically that the sounds were only derivatives of dying vibrations passing through the time barrier. In NowTime, sound passed behind the TimeWall and slowly dissipated with frequencies winding down the spectrum; soft, haunting sounds calling him. Surprisingly, he was running out of time. His first attempt at breaking through the TimeWall was successful, but left him confused with strange recurring memories, broken equipment, and no evidence except his word. His father's gift of a bus pass would soon expire and if he didn't use it, he'd be stuck at home, with his mother complaining about his lack of friends, a job, or romantic life.

José Isaac Davidovich's ambitions continued to nag him, and the recurring dreams of his past the Shadows had implanted didn't help any. He knew that the first person to cross the barrier and return with evidence would be feted in his small group of scientists-explorers. The lecture circuit and its glory, along with facetious discussions and marginal food awaited. An honorarium or even University tenure was in the mix. His status as 'first' meant that his opinions mattered slightly more than those who came after his success. It sounded great and he could have lived on the educational talk circuit, but his lack of an advanced degree locked him out of that lucrative sideline for the most part.

It took hours of scrounging to find the replacement parts he needed and he was beginning to wear out his welcome at the local electronic and TV repair shops. The mall rent-a-cops were on the alert and he had to contend with them, rats and the homeless for access to the dumpsters. Despite the impediments that non-scientists and rodents threw his way, he managed to rebuild his time-breaking backpack.

It looked like RadioShack® was going out of business, his source of cheap electronics. A trip around the country using his papa's bus pass could be a source of found electronics from the marginal TV repair shops located in most small towns. He was going to give his TimeWall device one more try before hanging up the dream for a while. A free bus trip around the country would be an excellent use of resources as he searched for spare parts to build a better machine.

José went over his equipment. It was a box attached to a metal frame he built in his shop class. Speakers covered the front, a few tweeters, subwoofers, and a sound bar he extracted from discarded equipment. Inside the box were amplifiers, boosted with capacitors and tuned with adjustable diodes. A battery pack filled the bottom of the box and vacuum tubes stuck out the top, like a set of rabbit ears. A small oscilloscope borrowed from his high-school electronics class let him visualize and tune the sounds in real time.

Technology had improved since the last time he used the TimeWall instrument and an array of multi-mode sensors tied into a small hard drive would record his trip and prove his ability to open the TimeWall.

His study of the dying sounds bleeding through Time sent him to what passed as wilderness near his basement lab. He couldn't avoid all extraneous noises, but racing motorcycles and buzzing cars interfered with the sensors strewn around his backpack.

José was ready to face the past, searching for a chorus to sing a hole in the fabric of history. Sensors captured barely audible tones as noise vibrated through the TimeWall and died, the present becoming past.

He was up before dawn and tossed his backpack in the rear of his mom's ancient Oldsmobile. He shifted the car into neutral, quietly rolling into the street. Once well away, he fired up the engine and drove to the outskirts of town, dodging questions and incrimination.

He drove his mother's car to the local Lover's Lane, partway up the rolling foothills above town. The turn-out was empty as the sun rose, framing the knoll covered with a wild lawn of grasses and sedge, touched with a sheen of morning dew. The only signs that someone had been there were cigarette butts, empty beer cans, and miscellaneous plastic debris carelessly tossed in the dusty turnout as mementos of successful dates.

His trip up the small hill was marked with a trail of crushed plants and wet shoes. José stood in an isolated field, far from the hustle and noise of modern civilization. It was important to record his work for prosperity, or until the TimeWall passed his location and covered up the results.

The location and time of day protected him from intrusions and lowered the risk of an embarrassing public failure. José activated a small radio-controlled helicopter he built from a kit and modified to record his trial. There was always a chance the RC toy would drift off, so he drove a tent peg into the soft soil and tethered the copter to it.

It took a bit of work to activate the backpack as the copter recorded his every move. Sensors picked up every sound, including when he was talking to himself.

"I'll take a video of the equipment as a memento before I start. Let's see if these new sound patterns make a difference. I'm close to a solution, I know it."

There was no need for an affirmative speech or a fancy *adieu* to friends, family, and the world. He tried and failed so many times; congratulations before results would be ridiculous. A simple, "Time to get started," was all José said, ignoring the pun. He looked back to make sure the copter was facing the right way and wasn't moving from its assigned place.

"Here goes nothing!" He flipped the switch and the manufactured banshees began their terrible songs. The pitch varied and sound levels fluctuated, looking for the exact frequency to welcome Time to the neighborhood. Banshee wailing up and down the spectra pushed at the TimeWall, trying to force it into the visible spectrum. Anyone watching the action would see a teenager hunched over, with a huge backpack, spitting wails of pain and concern.

Air quivered, standing waves danced, and Time responded. It only took a moment before the TimeWall appeared, extending beyond the edges of known space and through Earth. It shimmered, colorful Time bubbles pulsating to the beat of history. A small piece of endless time may have opened as our young scientist disappeared.

If anyone was watching, they didn't know if he succeeded or if the noise generators shook him apart at the molecular level. The closed TimeWall knew the answer, and it wasn't talking.

Chapter 15 -
Time to Break-In

"Eureka!"

"I made it. Let's hope it goes better this time. No way I'm going to be pushed back. I'm sure my replicants aren't going to attack me. They've had time to adjust and should be nicer, even though I forgot to bring candy."

Time marches on and leaves our wandering scientist looking down the past, where a thin line of replicas trails off to the horizon. The moving time-wall he passed through sends living shadows in a never-ending line of succession.

Everything is a one-dimensional duplicate of the world beyond TimeWall's bubbling Jello-like interface. It's an ever-repeating trail of static ghost echoes that displays local reality as slices of rocks, plants, insects, and vertebrates.

Each distinct entity is connected to its host outside the barrier, a slinky of time-slices becoming history. Every move of the source shifts the slice's focal point in an intersecting dance trailing off as far as the eye can see. Each item appears to excrete a soft gray fog, consigning the whole environment to a surreal appearance as it slowly dissipates into the void.

In theory, he could go back down the path of Time's history, but he had no option to advance beyond the TimeWall, although lateral and tangential movements seemed to be possible with little effort.

Maybe if I stay here long enough, my past will catch up with me, and I can change things, José thought.

The TimeWall solidified at his back. He turned and pushed, trying to face the wall of an unyielding past.

He knew the theories of time, all of them. After all, he was an expert on its permutations. He was determined to take control of Time's path and destination as much as an insignificant sentient could.

Time-bubbles sparkled and shimmered while colorful, rich bits disconnected from the moving wall, shining in the distance, tempting the unsuspecting traveler to *schlep* down new directions. He licked his lips, sampling the sparkling surroundings, and immediately regretted it, as it tasted like moldy, electrified air.

An electric arc, a bolt of power, was always a risk if a traveler stayed too long in one place. Time was not alive and not thinking, yet it reinforced the command to move forward or be turned into elemental particles.

The invisible, unknowing barrier stood as a monument to its actions. Committed, completed, and unchangeable. There was no break he could discern. He could neither go over nor under the hindrance.

Each time-slice contained his world, frozen and inaccessible before rotting and dissolving as the wall of Time-bubbles moved forward.

Sure, solid pieces -- bones, metals, and plastics -- could be examined by future paleontologists and a past life determined, but those pieces were only the dead husks of the former living.

If he was a wizard, he could cleave the wall with his magic wand and cast an exquisite time-spell, then step back behind the veil to exit this world. But magic isn't real. He would have to fall back on his scientific skills to find the instrument that would help him.

He knew violating Time's rules could have dangerous and unforeseen consequences, but this was his life's work, and he had to find an answer.

Sounds made in the Now could creep beyond the barrier, vibrations impinging on the now-solid invisible force, carrying the past and marching toward the future.

He had a virtually unlimited amount of past to discover. It was self-generating and self-blocking with little or no intervention by humans or the rest of the universe for that matter. Localized time may seem static, but it is perceived as running at different speeds depending upon observation and location.

A gnat, beating its wings in mating swarms, plays a tune only they understand. Each moment is a fraction of a wing stroke as they compete for mates and status. Humans think these midget insects live fast and die young, while gnats have a full life filled with adventure, entertainment, sex, birth, and death. It is, after all, relative.

Every piece of reality stretched forward, a QTmBit interval apart, except for his line of succession. His view, blocked by a slice of his image, was part of a line of Shadows. All of the other slices made of trees, grasses, insects, and more, continued to lengthen, connected to the moving time wall he just came through. He faced his image, frozen, not following the rest of TimeWorld's slices.

"I hope I didn't break anything," José said. "Although I don't see how facing my image can be of any consequence."

As he stood up, his me-slice shook, throwing off a puff of fog, and faced its host, mimicking José's every move.

"Is this me?"

The line of simulacrums, created as unique scenarios of his timeline, stopped and stared. Their host, who was sitting in the grass where he fell as the time-wall opened up, now stood facing them. The lead simulacrum was stuck at the front of the line with no host connection, never refreshing.

"What is this place? Is it Time?"

No one replied and sounds echoed as if in a vast foggy canyon. He wasn't expecting an answer from these images, but talking helped him deal with the situation. The only sounds around resembled a soft wind, transmitted from the Now and rapidly dropping off in amplitude and frequency as it fell in Time.

"It's like looking in a dark mirror."

The mirror person's edges were not sharp but fuzzy, lightly smoking. José's doppelganger looked confused until it connected to the new reality of a differentially placed host. It stood in front of José and shifted with him as he moved to check his history. The Shadow block kept him from seeing the extent of the situation.

"Strange. Every time I move, my Shadows block me. They won't let me see around."

He took out his trusty mirror and taped it to his selfie-stick.

"Okay, now I see what's going on. I wonder if my history goes all the way to the beginning of Time? I should check that out, I'm sure it will be an interesting journey."

He twisted the mirror and looked down the line of linked visages. They were thin, the thin of one-dimensional aberrations. Connected with flexible QTmBits, molecular fog separated every time slice, ensuring they could not quite touch the one before and after.

"This is one unusual conga line. If they start the hokey-pokey, I'm gonna run."

The front-facing sidekick smiled. His pale gray skin and thick glasses looked almost identical to its ancestral source. Each slice was lighter, becoming more translucent as the line progressed to the distant horizon. The foggy edges made it difficult to see where one Shadow started and another ended.

"Well, that's one way to lose a few grams. Although being one-dimensional could cause some problems."

The questions were rhetorical but seemed to be taken seriously by his extensions. They began shaking, looking down the length of Time, wondering how far they had strayed without new Shadow-slices.

Chapter 16 - Time to Talk

A distant snap, a dim fog cloud rising in the distance, answered as the line of slices pushed forward in a standing wave of Shadows. His past crested in front of José and the leading time-body seemed to grow in stature; not size, but depth. His Shadows flashed and changed at each condensation event. Each strike released a burst of fog and a slight noise; sharp, flat or whooshing, as if sound drove the time experience.

The faces changed with each contracting Shadow, singing a song of his past. Some were happy, some sad, and a handful appeared angry. The shrinking stopped and a single face stood out from the rest.

"Is that the sound of my life?" said José. "It isn't like any tune I've heard before."

José stood, waiting for the next move, time passing. A sound, not melodious but not unpleasant either called his attention as an overly loud, rude voice asked,

>What are you doing here? You're out of Time.

José always tried to be honest, and lying to his selves would probably be self-defeating.

"I stepped through with my time-noise generator. It cut the TimeWall like a knife. Now here I am, José Isaac Davidovich, TimeExplorer."

There was a slight change in facial movement, the faces flipping like a deck of cards. Not from muscles, but as if another time frame took charge as a slightly different tone rang out selecting a visage.

The new face, angry and accusing, all but shouted.

>And who gave you permission to crack the TimeWall?

"No one. I'm a scientist. I test things and make conclusions about what I find."

New tones wafted in the dense fog, faces flipping and a sardonic look became the front Shadow's face.

>Oh? So, you don't need rules? How lovely!

The Sardonic Shadow and the Shadows in aberrance puffed up with success, proud of their skilled *bon mot*, and waited for a reply.

Do I sound like that? Maybe these pieces are modified. Surely I'm not that obnoxious?

"As a matter of fact, I don't need your rules. My experiments lead me on as I go. *Cogito, ergo sum.*"

His replicated form looked at him with a slightly twisted, quizzical face.

José said, "You wouldn't know about that. You're only static pieces of what was me. Can you even think?"

A somber tone echoed and died in the empty time-space as a sad, reflective face stared at its host.

>We are you, and you are us. At least we're consistent in our time-slice.

"Not from what I can see. Now clear out, I want to explore as much as I can, as time allows."

Easier said than done. He was still missing a suitable tool, his "magic wand" to dismiss his replicants.

"Well, this is a fine pickle. I hadn't expected to see so many me's in the past. Maybe I can reset the controls on my backpack and blow these pieces of me away and start over."

The leading face became a frown, changed its tune and with a worried expression said,

>If you blow your past away you'll become an empty shell. We wouldn't recommend it."

"It's hard to argue with myself. I should know better. By the way, aren't you disconnected from your past history? I bet that feels strange."

Before he could devise a plan, the lead Shadow turned around and the string coalesced, pulled and squeezed back to the breaking point, trying to rejoin their past in a disharmonious expression of defeat.

"I guess I won that argument. Take that, Me!"

Deep down, he knew that fear of abandonment was the key to sending his Shadows scurrying back home.

The surroundings were constantly filling in and moving at Time's pace, except for the empty space of his replicants, who seemed to be stuck in the distant past.

José continued to talk to himself, if for no other reason than to fill the moldy, foggy air with a human voice.

"I better get out of here. My me's seem stressed. I'm sure they'll reboot once I get back to the Now. I'll come back later with a plan."

José looked around. Staying in one place didn't seem normal in this time-world as strings of newly created rock and tree pieces pointed to the exit. Time moved forward and he had to catch up with the barrier.

"I better get moving. Who knows what would happen if I became stuck behind Time?"

To add insult to injury, the TimeWall was moving and he had to walk to keep up with Time's pace.

"I shouldn't have worn my new sneakers. I think I'm getting blisters. All this walking hurts my feet and this backpack isn't getting any easier to carry either."

His pace was leisurely to start. He could see the TimeWall in front of him, but he didn't seem to be making progress, Time was always moving faster than he could walk. José began to jog to get to Time's leading edge.

Worrying thoughts broke through the fog. *At least time's not running out. I wonder how much I have to complete this journey? What happens if I can't leave? Will my history be destroyed? Will I be forgotten in an instant? I should have talked more with my past Shadows. They've been here longer than I have. They must know what's going on here.*

Fortunately, rocks, trees, and dirt don't change much in the short time he was in Time's world. It was hard enough to walk fast without worrying about tripping over miscellaneous junk popping up in his path.

"Finally," José exclaimed. "I can see the leading edge of the barrier, and it's still daylight."

The shimmering time-wall called his name, unless he misheard the soft banshee-like screams of dying sound waves.

The closer he got to the leading edge of time, the more resistance he met. Time-Jello was not his friend going forward. He reached the edge and pushed at the TimeWall, but the persistent Jello was skinned over and he couldn't pass.

64

"This would be so much easier if I had an instruction manual," José muttered. "I wonder if any other researchers have made this journey? They should have told me what to expect. Maybe they left me a message? How would that even work?

He could still see the barrier as the sun set in the Now world. Light dimmed, then turned off, replicating the physical space of the outside world. Behind him, there was a distant glow from Time's passage as ancient days and nights merged in the distant past.

"This is not getting me anywhere. No matter what I do, Time is always one step ahead. And I'm tired."

Muttering to himself did no good and he thought, *Well, I'm in the dark on how to resolve this, but I can't stay stuck here forever. Right?.*

Chapter 17 -
Time to Hunt

José's Shadows finally caught up with their host, stopping a respectable distance away.

"Well, this is fun. I suppose my Shadows are expecting me to tell them what to do. It's not like I control them."

The forward-facing Shadow shook its head.

"Well, maybe I do. This is weird, I can't just stand around looking at imitations of myself," said José.

>What were you expecting, an e-ticket to visit the world's past?

"No. I don't know what I was going to find. So far it's been a big nothing-burger."

>So you think we're nothing? Without your past, you have no future.

"Who told you that? It sounds like something you'd find in a fortune cookie or a sci-fi book. It's pretty much meaningless. What else can you do?"

>You forget, we're you. What do you want to do?

José was stumped. All he wanted to do was break through the TimeWall. He never thought of what he would do after that.

"Okay. Fine. I've got it. It's my job to give you impetus."

>Anything you do will be mirrored here in Time, but you're the time expert. If you don't know, who will?

"I suppose if my line intersects others, we could query the connection," said José.

>There you go. We knew you could figure it out.

"Fine. Let's try something easy. Go back to the Timeless BBQ and find my *tio,* Carlos."

>Then what?

"I don't know. Say hi and look around."

>You mean spy on the other TimeExplorers?

The front slinky turned and consulted with its neighbors.

>We can try. Don't move, unless you want to lose your whole past.

"That might not be a bad thing," said José. "I could reboot my life and start over."

>Or become an empty shell of yourself.

"Again, that might be okay," said José

His front Shadow puffed out a whiff of fog.

>A zombie?

"Since you put it that way, maybe not. I'll stay here and wait."

His Shadow didn't have a fancy rejoinder ready, so José took the initiative and said, "One more thing."

>Yes, Columbo?

"Funny. Is that the best you've got? Anywho, tell me, how far can you travel down the past to the cross links? Can you find a famous person?"

>We don't know. We've never tried it before. Maybe we can find your papa?"

"Really?"

>The operational word here is 'try'.

"Well, maybe not this time," said Jose. "Papa may not be someone I want to talk to right now."

His Shadows turned inward and showed José a blank slate as they searched for ancient memories. The whole line started shaking, fog exhaled from every molecular pore, drifting off to become one with the fetid background.

"My Shadows are starting to vibrate, and they seem a little stressed out," said José. "I wonder if they're shrinking, too? Are my memories going to weaken when their molecular fog dissipates?"

José called out, "I hope you Shadows aren't losing my memories!"

The blank faces did not respond, not that José expected acknowledgment.

Maybe this wasn't such a good idea, thought José. *I know what I can do. I could bring some old plastic bread bags next time and capture the fog. Even if it won't save my memories, it would be fun to test it out in the lab. I wonder if my Shadows would mind if I stuffed one of them in a bag, too? I'd probably have to promise to bring it back, but it would validate the study.*

The TimeWall moved further away as José stood still and his Shadows attempted to connect with his *tio's* molecular-thin line.

"They better hurry. I wonder what the Speed-of-Time is? Will they get there and back before I lose access to the TimeWall? If too much time passes I might never find an exit."

His Shadows rippled, each one turning back toward José in a Busby Berkeley-choreographed sequence.

This is weird, thought José. *I wonder where they picked up that trick? Do they watch old TV shows when I'm not around?*

>We found him, although we didn't make it back to Timeless BBQ. It was too hard to travel that far.

>Your *tio* says 'Hi.' He was eating a burrito at your mom's Saturday get-together.

"How underwhelming," said José. "That wasn't the TimeSlice I was looking for. In fact, I was hoping for something more profound. Did you see my Papa anywhere along the route? Did my *tio* mention anything about Time or Jesus or something?"

> It's not like you gave us explicit instructions. In any case, we didn't go in that direction. It was hard enough to flip back and communicate with another line. The only reason it worked was that you and your *tio* have so many touch points. We can try again if you want to take the risk.

José noticed that his lead Shadows were pale and a little more dispersed.

"You don't look well," José said to his Shadow. "Is there something wrong?"

>Yes. It takes a lot of energy to flip backward.

"What sort of energy? Is it from me? Will you regenerate? Are my memories weaker now?"

>How would we know? That's your department. Why do we have to keep reminding you that you're the time scientist? Or is your memory shot already?

"Of course. I'm a time scientist. How could you think anything else? My memory is unaltered."

His Shadow blinked, another face coming to the foreground, but said nothing.

"Let me think," said José as he considered the last sandwich he ate on the other side of the TimeWall. "Who remembers turkey on rye with pickles, onions, and Dijon mustard?"

One of the Shadows in the line lit up and waved.

"Oh yes, and mayo. I guess I'm okay. No worries. I have all my memories."

The faces flipped. Sardonic Face led the way.

>If you say so.

José sighed. "Maybe we won't try that again anytime soon."

>Good idea.

No help from his string of Shadows, again. José thought, *It really seems that my Shadows get stupider the longer I talk to them. Maybe I should give them an IQ test to set a baseline.*

"I mean, what could I do with that memory anyway? It's not like my *tio* is going to walk up here and share his lunch."

>Now you're learning. We can contact your past and ask what you want, but it isn't without cost to your memories and probably your mind. Use us with caution.

"Message received," said José. "I won't try to find any other connections like Napoleon or Kevin Bacon. Anyhow, it's getting late. I've learned everything I can for now."

>Yes. Please leave.

Faces flipped. Worry was in charge.

>If you're here after dark, the *Chupacabra* can attack us. You need to leave.

"The what? Are you talking about a myth? Maybe I better stick around and see it. Think of the paper I could write if I found one."

>Cryptids are a myth on your side of the TimeWall. Here they are real and they can be dangerous. Think of your memories being torn from your soul. Please leave.

José was unfazed.

"Are there other cryptids here? Maybe you can find Bigfoot? Better yet, Nessie, or do we have to go to Scotland first?"

His closest Shadow shook his head and ignored the stupid question.

José said emphatically, "I'm not afraid of a goat-sucking myth. How could a cryptic dog hurt me? None of my memories are goat-shaped."

His line of Shadows could have done a facepalm, but that didn't seem to be part of their repertoire.

"If you're done tossing myths around, I'd like to top up the charge on the battery. I don't suppose you have a plug out here?"

The Shadows didn't even bother to flip for a new face.

"Yeah. I guess not. Don't go anywhere, I'll let you know when I'm ready to leave."

Chapter 18 -
Time to Jog

It was getting darker and a dusty overlay of mold and gut bacteria gases permeated the dank air. He could still breathe, but it was far from pleasant. Rings of day and night echoed down the past, giving everything a weird glow. The closer he was to the TimeWall, the darker it became.

"I wonder if there is anyone else here?" said José, hoping for an answer, but hearing none.

Lights shone in the distance, dimming as they traveled away from the time interface.

"Are these people? They must have lanterns. Or maybe there are houses with friendly folk and food. How do I contact them?"

José did what he hated most and started jogging toward the twinkle, his new shoes stiffly crunching against the constantly refreshed soil.

Before he ran out of breath, he closed in on the blinking light. *Maybe I should have spent more time at the gym. This time-world is no easier than the regular one. I'm sure I was in better shape when I had to ride my bike up here. Next time I'll bring it along.* He continued to speak out loud, and to himself, apparently, "This isn't right. It's only a tiny piece of Time's opportunity-Jello. I can't do anything with it."

The jello seemed stuck in the air, unconnected, not falling nor moving as it drifted backwards as time moved forward. Unused, unloved, and fading fast, the opportunities' glow would last until its eventual dimming oblivion.

"That's it. I can't take it anymore." He collapsed, becoming one with the fine gray dust and decaying grass. "This is not what I wanted. I don't seem to have any control. And my feet hurt."

His Shadows, who had been trying to keep up with their host, found their mark as he pondered his fate. The connected time remnants unwound and closed in on José.

71

He looked up to see his time slices staring down at him, reflected in the glow of past days. Sardonic Face seemed to be in control, again. José didn't know what his Shadows would do. *It can't be good,* he thought. *Are they going to crush me to end this farce? Or suck me into their matrix, becoming one-dimensional, gray, and past?* José stood up. If he was going to end his time on this shadow Earth, he was going to do it with pride and dignity.

Sardonic Face saw his confusion and said,

>Now what, Einstein? How's Time working out for you? Your little boom box opened up a hole, and you don't belong here.

José had been insulted by many people throughout his life. Classmate, teachers, friends, even his mother. But this was worse than he expected. He was being insulted by himself. The Shadows shimmered as faces flipped and emotions fought for control. Concern moved to the front.

>You must get out of here. If you stay, Time will rot your bones, and we're not ready for that.

The faces flashed again, and a young, deeper concern looked at its host.

José inspected the new countenance. "Oh, I remember that face. I sure do miss that hairstyle."

>I've always wondered what an older me would look like.

"Well, what you see is what you get, just me and a string of other me's."

>I don't mean to criticize, but when are you going to have any children? If you leave with no progeny, we'll be left all alone with no path forward.

"You sound like my mother. That can't be me talking."

>You just have to stay unattached, don't you? If you end, it will end us all.

"You don't know that. Maybe I have a kid somewhere or will in the future."

Sarcasm rang its bell and took a swipe.

>Sorry, Charley. If you had a child, it would be here along your stream. And we'll know if it happens in your future, we'll be watching. We want you to keep trying, or maybe start trying someday.

"That sounds a bit creepy. Do you have to watch?"

Sarcasm switched to a wry smile, José blushed.

A hyperactive scientist pushed its way forward.

>Think. You got us into this. Use your sound knife to get out.

"Of course." José didn't normally take advice, but this was different; it was from someone he knew and trusted, even if it was a one-dimensional Shadow. He quickly turned on his backpack's sound generator and inverted the tones.

The replicants shook to the point of dispersal, letting loose with a foul, loud multiphonic banshee howl.

"Glad those wraiths are with me. I'm sure they wouldn't hurt me. Without me, there is no them."

He kept at it, adjusting, tweaking, nudging an obscure assemblage of noise.

"They don't look happy," said José. "Or maybe that's just one of their fugue faces. Oh well, no pain, no gain, and I'm not feeling the burn. I'll up the volume and see if that opens the wall."

A crack, a mere sliver, appeared as the banshees and noise-generator merged and the ear-shattering cacophony became almost intolerable. His world flashed and he popped into real time, his symbionts disappearing from view.

José began talking to the air, trying to make sense of what had just happened. His sound-generating backpack looked the worse for wear, a small crack appearing in one of the vacuum tubes and the smell of overheated capacitors filling the air.

"That was close. I better write these settings down. I wonder where the helicopter is? Did the camera catch any of this?"

The RC helicopter was hidden in the tall grass, dead to the world, its battery drained and out of gas. Our brilliant scientist forgot to mark the location down and would have to stumble over it by chance.

Words and thoughts continued to spill out. "I have no idea where I am. Is this the same world I left, or has Time dumped me into another dimension?"

He looked around. It was dark and smelled funny. The lights from the city still shone and he could hear an airplane flying by.

There was no one around to see José, unkempt and stumbling in the dark. Words filled the empty space as José asked the void questions it couldn't answer.

"Well, at least it looks the same, except for the smell. Unless that's me? This trip down Time's path has been stressful, and I think my guts may have been twisted a bit. I better find some place to freshen up. My *madre* would ask too many questions, but I need to find her car and return to civilization. I hope the gears work the same as when I left."

"That's not all, the helicopter has the recording. I better find it. Look here. My watch is scrambled. I'm going to have to contact Timex®, it may still be under warranty. It's dark, so I've been lost out of my Now for at least a day. It would be nice to know what time it is. I wonder how long I was gone?"

José kept talking to himself, as if spoken words would be heard and the emptiness would answer back. "Where is that helicopter? It should be close to the TimeWall entrance. It's not like it moved in time. It had nowhere to go. I hope no one took it."

He took out a light and began a cursory search. The flashlight flickered, announcing expansion of the dark and its dangers. His watch kept on ticking and after an hour's search, José knew he wasn't going to find his gear tonight.

He was cold, sore, and a little worse for wear.

"Maybe I'll go over to my *tia*'s place. A little chicken soup and a nap would go good right now. She's always supported me and won't ask too many questions. I really didn't expect to move so far laterally. I could be kilometers away. Oh well, I'm sure the 'copter is safe here. No one comes to this area. I'll come back in the morning."

He took a bead on the town's lights and traversed across the grass to the road, then headed uphill to his car, ready to call it a day.

Chapter 19 -
Time for Dr. Jamieson

Professor Jamieson's reputation preceded her and over the years, it told new students to find another professor. She was pale with dark hair and an almost permanent resting scowl. The professor pushed aside a few gray locks and looked up from her tablet as a hesitant knock echoed in her office. Her piercing glare would normally stop any trespasser in their tracks, but the intruder was a newly minted grad student and didn't know better.

"Haven't you read the office hours? Get out and don't return until you learn how to follow directions."

"Sir...uh, ma'am. We have some important news."

"It's Doctor Jamieson," as she pointed to the placard on her door.

'Time Studies Laboratory,
Professor Jamieson, Ph.D., T.Mc.,'
'Office hours: When Time Permits'
*'Please request future meetings
in a timely manner,
in the future.'*

"Excuse the intrusion, Doctor. We received information about a time study by a rogue participant."

"What? Who?"

"We're not sure. Some kids found an RC helicopter laying in a field and uploaded the data to the socials."

"Socials? What is that, some new TV station?"

"No ma'am...er...Professor. It's private bulletin boards, sort of like CompuServe and AOL."

"Is that even legal?" said Dr. Jamieson. "Why would the government let unfettered communication clutter our youth with unregulated ideas? I bet they're communists. I'm going to have them investigated."

"They're just a bunch of kids," said the grad student.

Dr. Jamieson raised an eyebrow. "Kids? You're bothering me because of children and weird TV stations? Why aren't those brats in school? Instead they're running around causing trouble. Where are the parents, the truant officers, the police?"

"I don't know, ma'am, I'm new at the university."

"For the last time, it's Doctor. Get that straight if you want to stick around. Graduate students are a dime a dozen. You mean nothing to me and can easily be replaced."

"Yes, Doctor. I'm sending the stream to your computer. It's called 'Banshee Deletes Man'.

"Unlike you, I can read just fine," Dr. Jaimeson snapped. "You better not be wasting my time."

The hacked video began simply: a person wearing an oversized trench coat was standing in a field.

"Is this our rogue operator?"

"Affirmative. Watch what happens when he turns on the sound generator."

A handheld camera moved in closer, revealing the control panel and wires streaming out of the square backpack. The picture jiggled as it was attached to an RC helicopter, but not before the camera focused on a close-up of his face, black curly hair, dark skin, and thick glasses.

Dr. Jamieson reviewed the video. "How did you get this video?

"We heard about the video on the chat boards and one of the grad students hacked in and copied it

"Well, at least you lot are not completely worthless," said Dr. Jamieson.

"Thank you, Professor."

Professor Jamieson rolled her eyes and said, "He doesn't look familiar. I don't think I've seen him at any of our meetings."

"No, Doctor. We didn't find him in the university's database. He looks to be about 170 cm tall, weighing around 60 kg.

"We need to find out who that is. What else do you have on him?"

"Yes, sir…ma'am…Professor. The information is in my notes I sent to your computer."

"Interesting," Doctor Jamieson continued to review the stream, "but worthless. You better have something more than a selfie. I'm busy with my own studies. My Proton Time Gun design is almost ready for a field trial. I don't see anything like that here."

"Wait, Professor. He's about to activate the device."

With that, an intense wail started in the lower ranges of human hearing. The RC Copter was pushed back a meter and trembled, attempting to stabilize its flight from the verbal onslaught. The volume and frequencies bounced around the spectrum, apparently searching for something.

"Great, a noise maker," said Dr. Jamieson, "I remain thoroughly unimpressed. Any kid can build a boom-box. If he starts dancing, I'm out."

With that, the surrounding air picked up the song, and floating dust, pollen, and water vapor responded.

"Oh, great. We know he can make air dance. Still not impressed."

"Yes, Doctor."

A thin line, a crack, not dancing, opened.

The poor student almost pleaded, "Please watch."

The crack widened, and the person disappeared in a poof of nothingness.

Professor Jamieson pulled back from the screen. "That's different. Unique even. It could be jump editing. How do you know this video hasn't been manipulated?"

"We've been working on it in the lab. Five graduate students and two techs analyzed the stream. They focused on a thousand unique blades of grass, and not a single one twitched. It was a smooth transition. There is no cut."

"He could have walked out following his old footprints. Did you check that?"

"No. We haven't had a chance to figure out the location yet."

Dr. Jamieson brushed by the grad student, talking to anyone who would listen.

"I'll send the video to my benefactors in the military," said Dr. Jamieson. "They're sponsoring the research, it wouldn't be too big of an ask to have them locate our quarry. They have maps and links to everything."

Geoff, the senior grad student, broke in to defend his team, "Good idea, Professor. You think of everything. We'll get on it."

The other grad students rolled their eyes, making sure the professor wasn't looking their way.

"One of my military contacts should be able to get a fix on the coordinates and the operator," said Dr. Jamieson. "There are some satellites that may have passed over and taken a picture."

One of the grad students said, "Really, Dr. Jamieson? I hadn't heard about those before."

"And you better forget about it, too. They are secret and I may have said too much," said Dr. Jamieson.

"That's okay, professor. I think one of the students is extrapolating that information from the surrounding terrain."

"You think?"

No response, but she knew the implications.

"Well, it seems you didn't waste my time after all."

Dr. Jamieson looked up as the student let out an audible sigh.

"Assemble a crew. I want every sensor we have. There must be a time signature somewhere. Find it."

"Yes, Doctor."

"Check his trail. See if there are footprints going back from the site."

"Yes, Doctor."

"And find out who that person is. We need to check his lab. Break the door down if you have to."

"Don't we need a warrant?"

"We're scientists. What on earth would we do with a warrant?"

"Yes, Ma'am. We'll be ready in 10 minutes."

"Make it five."

The professor turned, locked her office door, and walked across the hallway to help the lab rats gather their equipment. It was her laboratory and micromanaging was a skill developed over years at the university.

"You over there, check the databases."

"We already did, Professor. We can't get a firm ID, and the databases haven't been updated for this year."

"I can't accept that result. We need a name to go with that face."

A senior grad student offered, "Maybe we can call the police and report a missing weirdo with a backpack?"

Dr. Jamieson glared and shook her head. "Don't dare call the police. It could blow up in our faces. Think before you talk. We don't even know who we'd ask them to find."

"Sorry, Professor. I was only trying to help."

"Everyone, pack up the gear and get a move on. Now," said Professor Jamieson. "Time is of the essence. You know your careers are on the line."

One of the graduate students bowed as he stepped out of the crowded room. "I'll get the van ready."

"This better not be another false alarm. The chancellor has been looking for an excuse to give our program the axe, and we need to show him we're making progress."

The professor grabbed her go-bag and tossed in a few sensors her students overlooked.

She took one more review of the video stream, looking for anything out of place. *How did we let a rogue actor get the best of us? This'll be bad if we don't find him.*

Chapter 20 -
Time for a Couch

The sun peeked through the living room window and gently woke José from his perch on his *tia*'s couch.

Was that a dream? The first time I broke through the TimeWall, my memories were seriously trashed. I can't tell my tia *about it. She probably thinks I'm crazy already. She'd blab to my* madre *and maybe my* tio. *I best keep this to myself until I check the cameras and recorders.*

He got up, dressed, and spoke to the bedroom door, "*Tia* Rose, I have to get back to work. Thanks for the couch and chicken soup." There was no response, but she was a heavy sleeper. He wrote a quick note and went on a search for his missing equipment.

He drove up and parked, ready to find his missing proof. This was his chance to show the world and beat the competition. The small turnout leading to the scenic trail was almost full as José found a spot. *There sure are a lot of cars here so early. I don't recall seeing any ads for a medieval-times joust. I better get my gear before someone else finds it.*

José huffed up the hill, still sore and stiff from the previous Time journey and the night on *Tia* Rose's uncomfortable couch. He quietly talked to himself, analyzing the situation.

"Oh my aching *tuches*, I'm such a *schmuck*. I should have never left without my equipment."

He heard voices ahead and the sound of banging metal and the hum of a generator.

"What are all these people doing around my spot, and what are those funky-looking devices? If they found my gear, they'll have my face on video."

He ducked below their sight line. "I don't see a TimeWall crack, so they can't do anything about that."

He was close enough to hear the conversations as they scurried about.

"Dr. Jaimeson," said Geoff. "We triangulated the location based on the uploaded images, but had no luck finding the recording device. There's a trail and an indentation from where it might have been set up. We're in the right place."

"Luck has nothing to do with it," Dr. Jamieson said. "Keep on searching. I bet those kids took it. Is there any way to track them?"

Geoff replied, "I'm afraid not. They shut down the bulletin board right after we hacked into their system. Their IP address was sent through multiple sites to hide their location. I guess they were afraid of the authorities."

"They better be afraid of me," said the Professor. "I'll contact the military and they'll find those thieving kids."

"I don't think they stole from us," said Geoff. "From what I've heard, they found it abandoned. They could have come from anywhere, the trails here are very popular."

The professor was not happy. She scowled and started to say something. The anger management course the university forced her to take kicked in as she counted to ten. No explosion, but no one would receive an 'A' for this field trip.

"Fine. It's all fine. See if you can find any time signatures, check 500 meters in every direction."

The team of students moved as far away from the professor as they could and still appeared as if they were working. "We're on it, Professor."

The crew unpacked boxes of antennas, sensor dishes, laser emitters, and goggles. They put on HazMat safety suits and trudged out to check for signs of…something.

They look like they're on a nuclear dump site, thought José. *I don't think they have an idea of what they're doing. So much the better for me.*

They used a random, fear-driven search pattern to cover as much ground as possible, without entering the professor's space. They searched high and low for anything they could use to report back. They weren't so much interested in getting a good grade as avoiding being kicked out of the university for wasting everyone's time and money.

José watched for a bit, satisfied that there was nothing to find, and considered his journey.

I better leave and check to see what I was able to record from the sensors on the backpack.

Staying out of sight, he walked down the hill to his parked car. The only thing to do was go back to his basement laboratory and figure out his next step. He had something every other time-scientist lacked and that was first-hand experience. As he drove back to his lab, he drew up conclusions and concepts of his experiment.

The time-slices were a descending slinky of one-dimensional snapshots tied the present to the past. Not only humans but each blade of grass, rock, or animal had their time-slices existing beyond the barrier. Each segment represented a QTmBit moment connected to the Now-Timeline.

He figured that anyone stepping behind the TimeWall would meet their linked pieces just as he had. His slinky Shadows were lost and confused when their benefactor ended up on the wrong side of Time. Their peaceful, quietly degrading existence was thrown into chaos and they chased their host around like a lost puppy, begging for the next connected hit.

Visiting the past could be unnerving, seeing all the time slices, each one a little different, static, and demanding reconnection. He knew that once the TimeWall was broken into, everyone would want to drop back and talk to the historical geniuses, shakers, and movers lost to history. That was obviously a folly.

Stepping beyond the barrier, humans were limited to their connected past. Time slices crossed and intermingled. The past lives of anyone not directly connected were distant and all but unreachable.

It was not only a connection problem but a time and distance issue. The past world might go back to the beginning of Time, but its depth ruled out any serious exploration of history.

It wasn't that there were no slices of automobiles or aircraft to speed the journey. The one-dimensional aspect of Time's hardware made it unusable for transport by three-dimensional hosts. Maybe he could figure out a way to jump over the recent past, but for now, his exploration was limited by nature and connections.

José knew that once other scientists figured out how to access the past, they would want to learn how to go forward. That was equally delusional. Forward time didn't exist until it became.

They could push against the limiting Time-Jello environment surrounding them, encompassing all actions, but there was no distant future beyond the immediate Now.

His theories could be true or false, but he had enough of trying to make sense of what he experienced and headed back to his lab to look at the facts encoded on his equipment. He closed and locked the door and sighed, "This is better than *schlepping* around the wet grass or the weird time world."

Paquito had nothing to do, the kitchen was closed, and joined his human buddy in the lab.

"Paquito, you can give me a paw. Let's pop open the cassette and see what they have to say."

José opened his backpack, carefully extracted the tape and wound it back with a pencil before plugging the cassette into the tape deck.

"I'll extract the data to the computer's drive first, then upload it to my CompuServe account. There is only so much you can do at 300 baud. I don't want to risk a hardware failure."

Every card, and every sensor report was a fuzzy gray fog.

"It's all noise. I've got nothing here. It's the same as last time. No one will believe me without hard evidence."

He sat, head in hand trying to make sense of the information. "I bet the cards got wiped passing the time wall. I should have checked the recordings before I returned."

The scientist, optimistic as always, took every failure as an opportunity, trying to reason out a solution. He was not willing to be denied so easily.

"I know what. I need to do it again with better cameras and a wider sensor range or maybe wrap everything in tinfoil before exiting. I need to check the dumpster behind the TV shop, maybe hit RadioShack® again, although they never seem to have what I need."

"I'm sure the next time, I'll have it all worked out. I should check AOL to see if there is any gear I could trade."

Chapter 21-
Time for a Bus

José was at an inflection point. His last trip beyond the TimeWall mangled critical components and he was at a loss on how to get new supplies. His local contacts didn't pan out and he needed fresh dumpsters to explore.

Thankfully, his papa's bus pass allowed him to travel without spending a lot of money. Exploring ancient TV and radio repair shops was his goal. With a little luck, he could stock up on material for more TimeWall machines.

José was one of the lucky ones. The combination of electronics, wood, and metalworking skills proved easy to translate into paying jobs in any city rolling under the bus's wheels. He routinely hit every RadioShack™ and independent TV/radio repair shop he could find, looking for cheap, ancient, and unloved components.

The arrival of boxes of cast-off electronics and miscellaneous parts was the way his mother kept track of where her son was, postmarks supplying locations but not necessarily timing. She dutifully stored the boxes in the basement after searching for gifts and trinkets her son may have included by mistake.

He had nowhere to be and was free to dangle in the wind until the bus pass expired. This was time to ponder his future, one bus depot to the next. The pass let him jump off anywhere he wanted and catch the next bus whenever he was ready to move on. Hitch-hiking supplemented travel between unconnected stations.

José continued collecting ancient vacuum tubes, resistors, and capacitors, paying pennies on the dollar for obsolete equipment.

He became an expert at reading schedules and plotting itineraries using maps found at the local libraries. He preferred small towns in out-of-the-way locations with well-defined core areas.

This stop was pretty much like all the small-town transit hubs. A covered porch protected the buses and passengers. The station was filled with plastic chairs, a news stand with candy and chips and a walled-off ticket stand.

It was the middle of the day, hot and humid, and José wasn't sure what to do next.

He went through his options: *I could go to the 'Y' and get a room, or take the next bus out, but to where?*

The ticket agent wasn't busy as José walked up.

"Excuse me sir, when is the next bus leaving?"

"We have lots of buses. It would depend on where you're going."

"Where do you recommend?" asked José. "Are there any sites to visit around here?"

"I'm not a travel agent, sonny. If you want to see the attractions, pick up some brochures or check the library. It's right down the street."

That was less than helpful, thought José. "Thank you, sir, I'll do that."

"Please do. Now, unless you're buying a ticket, you can leave. I have paying customers to tend to."

José looked behind and around. There didn't seem to be many customers clamoring for the agent's attention.

"Okay sir. I'll figure it out myself."

"Great," said the agent. "When you want to buy a ticket, I'll be here."

What a jerk, thought José.

He could have stayed a day or two, dropping meager dollars at the YMCA and local restaurants but chose to hop on the next bus out, to anywhere.

After a few hours traveling down county roads, the bus meandered up to a small nondescript town. There was a forced layover waiting for a bus connection, so José decided to spend a few hours looking around.

The main street had all the local community needs, stuffed into brick stores designed for window shopping. He made a mental note of the shops as the bus slowly made its way to the restaurant rest stop posing as the local bus terminal. Surprisingly, there was a TV repair shop between a barber and a pawn shop.

"Look at this," José said to no one in particular. "The trifecta. It has everything I need in this one block. Full-service TV repair shops are hard to find since the imports have taken over the market."

The proprietor of the TV shop stood in the doorway, waiting for potential customers to wander by. Hours spent on the bus taught José communication skills he never developed in high school.

"Good afternoon, sir. I'm passing through and was wondering if you need some help in your shop?"

"Go away. I don't let just any bum walk in and touch the goods. Didn't you mean to stop at the barber shop? We don't serve your kind here."

José sighed and made a guess from the sign and said. "You must be Tom of Tom's Quality TV and Radio. How long has the shop been here?"

Tom looked at the scruffy kid and thought, *Well, there's nothing else going on, I might as well pass the time, who knows, there might be some money in his pocket.*

"Tom was my father, I'm Tom Jr. We've been in the repair business since well before you were born. Are you looking to purchase a small radio?"

"No," said José. "I'm a repair person myself. Do you have anything you need help with?"

Tom Jr. looked up and down at José; skinny, nerd glasses, unkempt hair, a beat-up backpack, and dusty shoes.

"What do you know about repairing TVs and radios?"

"I can fix just about anything that plugs into an outlet. I see you have an RCA Victor TV in the window. Does it work?" José stepped into the shop to get a better look and said, "It's model CTC28. The cabinet looks a little beat up, but I can polish it and get the CRT working, as long as it isn't cracked."

Tom thought, *I have nothing to lose. If he can fix it, I can sell it.* "Tell you what, if you can get the TV running and clean up the cabinet, I can find a buyer. I'll split it with you 70/30, less any hardware you need to buy."

José had time to glance around the shop and saw some old SSB HAM gear gathering dust and the exposed guts of old TVs, with their vacuum tubes hanging out in the cold. He thought, *There's enough old gear here to rebuild two TVs, this job should be a piece of cake.*

"I have a better idea. I'll fix it, at cost, in exchange for some of your old vacuum tubes and HAM gear."

"Deal," said Tom Jr. "I got the HAM rig at an estate sale. The old man's widow was happy to see the stuff hauled off. There's no market for obsolete amateur radio gear. You can have as much as you want as long as you take it away. Do you have a truck? I'll throw in the antenna mast tower for free."

"No truck, but I'll check out what you have and ship anything useful home. My mother loves getting surprise boxes."

"It would be a surprise, that's for sure," said Tom Jr.

"I'll have to pass on the antenna," said José. "I could cut it up for scrap if you want. The metal should have some value. Do you have an acetylene torch?"

"No," said Tom Jr. "But I can borrow one. If you can cut it up into manageable pieces, I can have my brother haul it to the scrap yard. You'll have to split anything you get with him."

It broke José's heart to see useful gear scrapped, but there was no way to ship a 50-foot metal mast intact. He never got into HAM radio. Morse code wasn't hard to learn, but spending time chatting to the ether never interested him.

"Okay," said José. "It seems a waste of good metal, but HAM radio operators are few and far between.

"When can you start?"

"First thing tomorrow works for me. I need to check into the 'Y' for the night."

"Tell you what," said Tom. "There's a cot in the back and there's a restaurant a short walk away. You're not afraid of dogs, are you?"

"You mean your old pit bull in the back? I'd be happy to spend some time with him, maybe take him for a walk."

"Fine. I guess. But don't spoil him. No one is supposed to know he's friendly. Molossus, come over here and meet your new roommate."

Molossus stretched and stiffly walked over to meet his new friend.

"He's just like my mother's Chihuahua, Paquito," said José. "All dogs are basically the same. Does he like tuna fish?"

The next morning, José started in helping Tom. He was able to get the old TV running, replacing a few old vacuum tubes and tightening some loose wires.

"That's great," said Tom. "I thought that TV was going to be a coffee table. My dad hates the new TVs. This would look great in his living room. All he needs are a few of the over-the-air channels and a remote control to keep him happy."

"No problem," said José. "It was fun working on old tech. What else do you have that I can fix?"

"How long can you stay? I'm sure we can find something else to keep you busy."

"Not long, I'm afraid," said José. "My bus pass expires in a few weeks, and my mother needs my help. She's getting on in years."

"Sorry to hear that. You can stay as long as you want, but family comes first. I'll call my brother and he can pick up the TV. I'm sure my dad would want to see who fixed it. He wanted to work on it himself, but arthritis and bad eye sight got in the way."

"Glad to help."

"You two can talk about old equipment when we bring it over. It will make his day."

Chapter 22 -
Time to BBQ

Bus passes and summer only last for so long and José ended up back home before the first leaves of Fall. His mother wasn't feeling well and it fell to José to become the caretaker until she got back on her feet.

The basement was crowded with boxes of electronic flotsam stored in boxes sent from every town on José's bus trip. It would take a few weeks to sort and store his haul. José was in OCD heaven. He put on some gentle Gregorian chants, laid out a fine-grid notepad and began checking in the booty.

After a few hours, it was time for some food and to check on his mother. *I bet she'd like some nice chicken soup. I can open a can.* Nutrients and company are always welcome, even if his version of homemade soup lacked a little depth.

José checked his calendar, and the annual Timeless Barbecue was just around the corner. It was one of the few occasions when a crowd of introverted, OCD TimeExplorers could get together to exchange ideas, brag, and eat dubious food. José's mother would normally make a brisket for him to bring, but she no longer felt like cooking large meals.

There was no way for him to pick up the slack; he never learned how to cook since his mother was more than happy to do everything for her only son. He could have brought a bucket of chicken to the party, but that was considered *gauche*. Everyone was supposed to bring food to show off their best cooking skills. Points were earned if the food followed some cultural standard.

He couldn't come empty-handed and he didn't like beer. His expertise in cooking was TV dinners, frozen pizza, and the aforementioned fried chicken in a bucket, but none of those were exotic enough for the barbecue. As usual, his *tio* came to the rescue with enough home-cooked food for both of them.

Carlos drove up to the house in his latest acquisition, a red convertible sports car. The only passenger was a tinfoil-wrapped brisket buckled into the back seat. He beeped the horn, anxious to get to the festivities. José was glad to see that his current girlfriend was nowhere to be seen. It's not that he disliked his *tio*'s rotating girlfriends, but he had nothing in common and sometimes they weren't too bright.

José was looking forward to seeing other TimeExplorers and maybe finding some equipment on the swap tables. His contribution would be a few extra vacuum tubes he brought back from Tom's video repair shop. They would hardly be missed from his stash of found equipment. He knew that his main competitors, the universities and the military, would be there picking up whatever scrap of information they could find to advance their projects. The University used connections with industrial and military donors for research funds. The independents had the advantage here, since no one could figure out how to monetize a trip beyond the TimeWall.

Carlos's horn honking brought José back from his thoughts.

"Are you ready to go?" asked Carlos. "I've got the food, we're just missing you."

"I'm all set," said José. "Do you think Papa will show up?"

"Without your *madre* at the BBQ, he has no reason to attend," said Carlos.

"Yeah," said José. He hesitated and slowly said, "I knew that. I was just hoping he might show up anyway. I'm sure he knows I always attend the festivities."

"I don't think he knows about the party. How's your mother doing?

"She's fine, just a little slower and tired."

"I brought a plate of brisket. Do you think your mother will want it?" asked Carlos.

"I'll put it in the fridge. Maybe she'll eat it later," said José.

He ran up the stairs, placing the food in the fridge. "*Madre*," he called out. "*Tio* Carlos and I are leaving for the Timeless BBQ. I left a plate of brisket in the refrigerator. We'll be back before nightfall."

"That's fine," said Lara. "Say hello to Carlos for me. Maybe you can both come up and visit for a while when you get back."

"We'll do that."

José grabbed his jacket and joined his *tio*.

"Let's go, it's about an hour's drive to the Elks Club and I don't want to be late. Some of the other TimeExplorers will grab all the food if we don't arrive on time. It's as if they haven't eaten for a month."

"For some of them, it's probably true," said José.

José locked up the house. It felt like he was abandoning an old friend. Without him tinkering in the basement it seemed a little lonely. The rock-walled basement's job was to stand by and watch over the near-empty shell. A pat on his way to the car reassured his mineral friends, if they even noticed.

The two drove through town with the top down. The smell of warm meat turned the heads of every dog along the road. The Elks Club was located near the golf course, at the far end of the town, tucked against the foothills surrounding the small valley.

The parking lot was full of cars and vans. More than one of the vehicles were ratty-looking and worn down. The vans that weren't being lived in, appeared cleaner and had the logo of the university emblazoned on the door. A few newer sedans were scattered throughout the lot. Their military plates identified their origin and intent.

The Time explorers were there to eat, brag, lie, swap stories, and discuss the latest hardware. Everyone made their way down the potluck buffet, then slowly mingled with their compatriots before self-selecting to the benches. They ended up grouped into their respective methodology leanings: sound, light, high-energy particles, and conjurers. The university and military joined any group that looked interesting, hoping to pick the brains of the explorers.

José migrated to the junk tables, where time-breaking gear was swapped. He was looking for particular vacuum tubes and miscellaneous electronics to help rebuild his burnt-out device. It wasn't a successful attempt. Either the equipment was not there or the other TimeExplorers didn't want to part with the good stuff.

"You should check out the wizards," said Carlos. "Maybe you've been going the wrong direction. I'm sure they'd love discussing the merits of magic vs. science."

"You're kidding, right? The magical people talk a lot, but it never seems to make sense."

"And science does?" said Carlos.

"You may have a point, but we can actually prove stuff."

"Just saying, you need to keep an open mind."

"So garbage can fall in? No thanks."

Chapter 23 -
Time to Parry

"Mind if I take this seat?" said a young man coming over with a beer and slice of brisket on his plate. José looked up and saw a tall, thin man with a full head of red hair and a thin beard. It was obvious he was part of the university's group. Carlos looked at José and nodded.

"Hello, my name is Geoff, I'm a grad student with the university's Time Studies group. I heard you talking about breaking through the TimeWall. Have you heard about Dr. Jamieson's work?"

José looked up from his plate, deciding whether conversation was more important than eating.

"Geoff, you say? My name is José and this is my *tio*, Carlos. I've heard about it. I'm not impressed with the methodology."

Geoff was thrilled that his new acquaintances got his name right the first time.

"Perhaps you don't understand the professor's work," said Geoff. "I'm not allowed to go into a lot of detail, but Dr. Jamieson believes only high-energy devices can break through the TimeWall."

José took a bite of brisket, savoring the mix of flavors. His *tio* had really stepped up his cooking game. It was almost as good as his mother's. "Some of us would disagree. Proton rays are too destructive to the TimeWall. I believe it would shred time and the repercussions could be dangerous."

"So, you do know about her studies?"

Carlos raised an eyebrow, but kept on eating, not willing to break into the discussion.

"I've read up on the work she's done. I don't think she would agree with my concepts."

Geoff said, "I understand. Dr. Jamieson doesn't appreciate having her ideas contracted."

"That's an understatement from what I've heard."

Carlos decided it was time to support his *sobrino*. "José doesn't believe in high-energy systems. He uses sound generators."

93

"And that works?" said Geoff. "I'd like to discuss that with you. Do you have a lab I could visit?"

"Not really, I'm more of an independent scientist. Wouldn't Dr. Jamieson be upset if she found out you were looking at a different method?"

"To be honest, she doesn't broach any disagreements, but she isn't here," Geoff replied, "I'm not a spy, I'm looking for knowledge wherever it is. Maybe you should join our lab, even become a student? You could easily get a PhD."

"What could that piece of paper do? I don't want to teach and I doubt if it would help me get a job," said José. "Tell you what, I'll think about it. By the way, how successful has the Proton Time device been? Have you seen the TimeWall?"

"Well, no. But we're close, I'm sure," said Geoff. "How about you two? Any luck breaking through Time?"

"Not me," said Carlos. "José may have had better luck."

"Let's just say I'm working on it. Evidence is hard to come by, but I'll be trying again soon. I need to find a few obscure parts for the generator and then I'll be ready to go."

"That's why you should join Dr. Jamieson's group. We have funding from the government and can always use someone with your expertise."

José looked askance at the young grad student. "Government money is fine until the bill comes due. I've heard they want to break through the TimeWall and use it to spy on their enemies or even attack them. I don't agree with that philosophy."

"Well, you know, the military is responsible for protecting us all and if we don't do it, someone else will use the TimeWall to attack us."

"I don't think you or the military understand the nature of things behind the TimeWall," said José.

"And you do?" said Geoff. "So you've been behind the TimeWall! What's it like?"

"I'm afraid I've said too much. I'm still gathering evidence before I can make any announcements."

"I'd like to help," said Geoff.

"And leave the university?" said Carlos.

Geoff frowned. He hadn't thought of that possibility. If he helped José, he would go against his major professor and he'll never get the coveted PhD.

"Tell you what," said José. "If you can find me some special vacuum tubes I need, I'll mention you in the paper when I present it to the world."

"Vacuum tubes? Isn't that ancient technology? I didn't think RadioShack® still exists."

"Nevertheless, those pieces are key components in my device. Maybe your military friends might have a supply, tucked away in some underground lair."

"Yeah. I don't think that's a thing," replied Geoff.

Carlos nodded; he knew where this was going.

"Can't you ask them?" said Geoff. "They're sitting at a table right over there."

"Sorry," said José. "I prefer to keep a low profile, but since you're already part of the university, they won't think twice about it."

Geoff looked over at the picnic table filled with military and a few civilians who looked like undercover agents. They looked back at the trio.

"Maybe I'll just keep on with my studies. I must be going. Best of luck with your experiments," said Geoff as he got up from the table to join the other students.

"Watch out for spies," said Carlos.

"And the military," said José.

"That went well," said Carlos. "Do you think there might be a hidden source of material the military is hiding? Maybe you should check out the university's Time Lab. I'm sure they'd appreciate your views on Time."

"I don't think I'm going to try to break into a secret military warehouse," said José. "That's a TV show, not real life."

"Fair enough," said Carlos. "Look, there's Hector, haven't you worked with him before?"

José looked around the room. Hector was talking to the military group, sharing a beer and laughing. He waved at José and came over.

"Did you try the brisket?" said Hector. "It's just like your mother's. How is she feeling? Better?"

"Thanks, Hector. My *madre's* doing as well as can be expected. *Tio* Carlos made the brisket this time. I'm afraid I didn't pick up the cooking gene from my family."

"Well, it's tasty. I'm glad the skill set is still operational," said Hector.

"I saw you talking with the University geek," said Hector. "Did he learn anything?"

"Geoff? Not so much," said José. "He didn't want to lose his chance for a PhD, and wasn't willing to try something different."

"His loss," said Carlos.

"I met some of the military crew, we were talking about old times. Did you know I was a Marine?" said Hector.

Carlos answered. "Yes, you seem to want to tell us every time we're here."

"Geoff implied that the military might have a stash of equipment that I might use," said José. "I know they're supporting the university Time studies, but I just don't trust that group."

"Wise," said Hector. "They'll steal anything they can get their hands on and claim it for the government. Did you know that I've been having some luck with the sound generators? I can send the specs for my setup if you want to try it."

"That'll be good," said José. "I'm still looking for some specific vacuum tubes. I may need to check out my sources in the Midwest. My last trip there wasn't as successful as I had hoped. I found a few pieces, but nothing that would help. Old vacuum tubes are hard to find."

"Let me know. If you find a source, save a few for me," said Hector.

"Will do. I'm planning a bus trip soon and we can trade information when I get back."

"Same itinerary as the first trip?"

"Sure, why not?" said Jose. "I already know the route."

"Take care," said Hector.

Chapter 24 -
Time to Haul

After the Timeless BBQ, José began a search in earnest for those special old electronics that would help his TimeWall device sing. He continued traveling around from small town to small town by bus.

Fortunately, he had no trouble finding work, which paid for the next leg of his journey. The few times he found old electronic parts that might work hardly made up for the time spent searching.

"This is getting expensive," said José. "I didn't realize that a three-month bus pass was worth that much. At least my papa gave me that opportunity the first time."

He budgeted for the trip, and found enough gig work to keep on going, but the gear he was looking for wasn't easy to find. Tired, poorer, and hungry, he returned, defeated in his quest for a source of old electronic parts.

Back at home with no job and no interest in higher education, José began tinkering in his workshop in earnest.

He was quite happy to decipher dying noises sneaking through the TimeWall. His *madre* and her nosy friends disapproved of a single man working on his own path and began asking questions. They did their best and set up blind dates with their marginally educated daughters. His skills at small talk did not work well over pizza and a movie and he considered hitting the road again.

His TimeWall device was still broken from his last attempt. It could make noise, and the vacuum tubes would glow convincingly, but the TimeWall never seemed to form. Modern electronics looked good, but there was something about ancient tech that made it all work as one cohesive, reliable unit. He began looking for interesting places to explore and try to find equipment to add to his collection.

José started talking out loud to hide the lack of the banshees he needed to guide him on his journey behind Time.

Paquito was there to listen and agree, but he was having trouble getting up and down the stairs.

"I wonder if Tom's video store is still open. I could take a straight shot and not waste my time hitting all the unproductive sites again. I should have written down the name of the town. I don't even know if there's still a bus line in that part of the country. Those tiny Midwestern towns can easily shut down and blow away in a stiff wind."

"I better find my first TimeWall model and write down the part numbers. Was it the vacuum tubes, the diodes, capacitors, or did I miswire something that worked?"

Travel was on his dime this time and a repeat of his earlier explorations became tiresome after a short while. Try as he might, José's wandering bug was losing its charm.

He finally found his special town deep in the prairie.

"I remember this place, the barber and pawn shop are still open, and look! There's *Tom's Video, Repair, and Boba Tea Shop.*"

I guess he's branched out, thought José. *Let's hope he still has some old gear I can root through.*

José walked into the shop and saw Tom behind the counter,

"What can I do for you, young man?" said Tom. "We have new flavors, if you're interested."

"No thanks," said José. 'I'm more interested in your video gear, especially early TV vacuum tubes."

"You must have noticed the sign. It's not really a TV repair shop anymore, I just keep it up for nostalgia. Some of the older residents like the consistency and I can always ship something out to a repair center if I need to."

"Is Molossus still around?"

"No. How did you know about him?"

"I'm José, don't you remember?"

Tom focused. The hours of seeing nothing but young boba drinkers dulled his senses.

"Of course! José. What brings you back here? Not for the dog I'm sure."

"Is he still here?"

"I'm afraid he passed, but we have some puppies."

"Puppies! I'll have to see them."

"See them? You can have one. Or more."

José thought, *I can't have another dog. Paquito hated my experiments, even with the custom headphones I built for him. What would I do when I go beyond the TimeWall? My mother can't handle a puppy and the noise would probably drive it crazy.*

Tom showed José his back room, beyond the boxes of tapioca balls and cheap flavorings.

"This is my type of back room," said José.

Tom replied, "Wait until you get to the TV section. You like old vacuum tubes, if memory serves."

The narrow hallway opened to a large room. Tom hit the light switch and rows of TV vacuum tubes flashed a faint hello through the dust covering their glass shells.

"This is great. How much are you willing to part with? I have cash," said José.

"All of it. I'm getting out of the video repair business. It's boba tea for me. Say… that's a great tag line. Thanks, José."

"*De nada.* I guess I'll have to rent a truck."

"Great. Pack up everything you want, help me recycle the rest, and we'll call it square."

"Perfect," said José. "I'll stash my gear and we can get going first thing in the morning."

"Let's hit the diner before it closes, my treat," said Tom.

True to a small town bus stop and diner, the food was a bit greasy, the coffee hot and the ambiance classic.

"Things are starting to look up here. The last few years have been hard with the mill closing down."

José sipped his coffee and asked, "That's a tough thing to come back from. What happened?"

"The state is adding a new junior college a few miles out of town. This place is already starting to look up."

"Just wait until the college students start overwhelming the town," said José.

"Exactly. 'Videos and Boba Tea, *It's Boba tea for me.*' I'm ready for the kids."

José said, "I've never had a boba. Is it good?"

"Who cares? The kids drink it and that's all that counts," replied Tom. "Say, didn't you say you were going to go to a university? How'd that work out? I bet you could teach at the new college."

"I've got a scholarship, but I haven't started. Anyhow, I'd have to think about it."

"Well, it will be a few years until the college is up and running," said Tom. "I have an idea, you can teach and work at my Boba shop to make a little extra pin money. That sounds great, doesn't it!"

José didn't need a lot of time to think about it. *It's time to make a graceful exit.*

"Thanks for the offer, but I have my lab at home and it would be impossible to move everything and start over."

"I understand, it's hard to let go. My grandma was like that. You don't collect newspapers and magazines, do you?"

"No. And I'm not a hoarder. It's all laboratory equipment. That's completely different from hoarding."

Tom grunted before taking another sip of his coffee.

The days flew past and the pair had just about cleared out the other hoarder's storage space. José was in hog heaven. He found a working tube tester and cataloged every unbroken tube before carefully putting it away. He had a stack of old electronics and, after recycling all the non-working gear, was ready to return home.

"Good thing I'm used to driving my mother's Oldsmobile, this box truck is just about the same length. All I have to do is watch out for low bridges."

Before he left, he checked for puppies. Not that he didn't like them, but stowaways were not something he wanted to deal with.

Tom, holding two puppies, waved as José drove away.

"Last chance for some new buddies. Take two, they'll entertain each other. No work for you at all!"

"Good-bye, Tom. Take care of the pups."

José almost crashed as he leaned over to wind up the passenger side window. He made sure he was going fast enough to avoid any flying puppies.

Chapter 25 -
Time for Uni

Once he got back home, he had a pleasant week checking the equipment and seeing what combination of electronics would open up his missing TimeWall. None of the hardware activated anything except the dust in the lab, so it was time to try a different tack. The scholarship offer was in his back pocket and he began looking at higher education as a way to improve his prospects and keep him interested.

The university in his hometown had a Time-Laboratory and his high competency scores got him in the front door. It was better than bus travel, but the small and noisy dorm rooms proved to be little different from the cheap hotels on the road.

The thought of spending a few years as an undergrad was appealing. He wouldn't be a lost soul on a bus and his mother wasn't there to tell him what to do. It would be a breath of fresh air. Weekends could be spent in his dorm room, or if laundry called, a trip back home to help his mother and listen to her take on the world's problems.

José spent little energy on undergrad work and convinced the administrators that it would be better to be part of the Time study group.

A few simple tests and discussions with the teaching assistants and tenured professors gave him a boost out of dull everyday student studies. He already knew how to read and impressed his professors with his math skills. José was labeled a savant by those who feared his intellect, weird humming and music choices. They were more than willing to fob him off on some other group.

In almost no time, José joined the graduate students in the shared lab under Professor Nancy Jamieson, renowned Time investigator.

"Pay attention, everyone," said Professor Jamieson. "We have a new student. His aptitude scores are fairly decent, not like some of you layabouts. Show him respect and maybe he can teach you a thing or two."

José had enough experience outside of the hallowed halls of the university and knew that this was not the best introduction. He pushed his glasses back and said, "Hello everyone, my name is José Isaac Davidovich and I'm happy to share my experiences opening the TimeWall and see what you are working on."

Professor Jamieson turned to her new student. "I'm sure José meant to say his theories. No one has broken through the TimeWall and my Proton Time Gun is the only valid Time option. Isn't that right, José?"

Before José could reply, Geoff interrupted, bowing ever so slightly to his major professor and said, "I've scheduled the meeting room for next week. I'm sure José will be ready to explain his theories and how they might support Dr. Jamieson's Proton Time Gun."

"Fine, show him around and see if he has any bright ideas you might use," said the Professor as she went back to her office.

The senior graduate student said, "Welcome to the Time Laboratory José. My name is Geoff, with a G. We can always use another hand. You'll find the work hard but promising."

"Yes. We met at the Timeless BBQ a while back," said José. "Was she serious about the Proton Time Gun? That seems to be a bit overkill. My work has been with sound, freezing the QTmBits and cracking the TimeWall."

"Oh, right, I remember. You were with Carlos? He's done some work for the Lab. I'm not sure which program he's in. Glad to have you with our group. Did you give up on your sound device?"

"Not really. I just wanted to see what your group had and see if we can merge the technologies," said José.

"Don't say that around the professor. She only wants high-energy solutions."

"That's right," said a second student. "The military is looking for a way to punch through Time so they can travel incognito and support our government's right to control Time."

José was taken aback. He never thought of using the TimeWall as a means of control. He was in it for pure scientific research, conveniently forgetting how pure research led to applied atomic bombs. He thought, *This group may not be the best organization to join. Oh well, maybe I can learn a few things and help them discover different methods. What could go wrong?*

"Wait a minute," asked another student, "What are QTmBits? Does the Professor know about them?"

"QTmBits are the name I gave to the connections between time slices. I saw them when I peeked through the TimeWall."

"That isn't possible. We're the only group that has approached the wall. Where did you get the funding?"

"Funding?" said José. "I did the work on my own. I can show you. Do you have any vacuum tubes? I can give you the specifications."

Some of the students snickered. "Vacuum tubes! What is this, the 1970s?"

Another student offered, "Only bodegas have vacuum tubes and ancient testing rigs. No one uses that technology."

"Unless you want to build a black-and-white TV from scratch, or get a burrito," laughed another student.

"Well, I guess vacuum tubes aren't strictly required. Do you have a couple of oscilloscopes? I can set them up and adjust the output."

"This I have to see," said Geoff. "There's a bench you can use over there. How much power do you need?"

"Not much. 100 amps should cover it."

"We're going to have to do some quick rewiring. Everyone, grab your tools and let's give this a try."

Geoff was in his element. Giving orders and using the micro-managing skills he learnt from his mentor, Professor Jamieson. He quickly got the team organized.

José collected miscellaneous electronic parts from around the laboratory. The pair of oscilloscopes would stand in for TV vacuum tubes.

"This should work. It might even be better than TV tubes. I can tune the oscilloscopes to the exact frequency I need," said José. "Everybody ready? Ear protection would probably be a good idea."

Geoff ordered, "Don't forget to put on your safety goggles, too."

José flipped the power switch and checked the 'scopes to manage power levels and frequencies. Adjusting the paired rheostats to generate that certain banshee scream he loved.

The noise became exponentially unbearable. Screams and-low frequency noise came out of the speakers.

Geoff yelled, "Is this normal? It seems a bit loud."

"Perfectly normal. My device uses the power of sound to bring up the TimeWall."

As he spoke, a thin, tenuous ribbon formed at the apex of the focused sound wave.

"See? There it is," said José.

"Where? I don't see it," said Geoff.

Another grad student said, "I see it, sort of. I'd thought it would have been bigger."

"Sorry," said José. "It's supposed to encompass the whole of reality, I guess this setup can't do it. Let me make some adjustments."

The oscilloscopes, angry at having to imitate vacuum tubes, made their feelings known by imploding.

José jumped back. "That's never happened before. I'm going to have to explore this phenomenon."

The door swung open, and Dr. Jaimeson stood glaring in the doorway. "What is all this racket? I was on the phone."

Geoff leaned over to José, "You may have a problem."

"Who did this?" shouted Dr. Jamieson.

Those who weren't deaf by now or could still understand words making their way past ringing ears, pointed at José, "The new guy did it."

"You're on report," said Dr. Jamieson. "One more stunt like that and I'll have you expelled."

"Yes, Professor," said José.

As she stormed out of the room, Geoff turned to José and said, "I'm impressed. Your testing scores must have been really something. Normally, she'd grab you by the collar and toss you out on the street."

Chapter 26 -
Time for a Baby Proton

The echo of a slammed door reverberated in the lab.

"Do you think I'll be thrown out of the program?" asked José.

Geoff thought for a minute before saying, "She might. You've got a federal grant, don't you?"

"I believe so. Whatever tests I took before I entered the Time Lab program came with some stipends."

"That explains why you haven't been shown the door after that stunt," said Geoff. "Dr. Jamieson won't kick you out as long as you're a source of funding for the project."

"I guess that's a good thing," said José. "I hope there was no permanent damage. I didn't expect it to get that loud."

Most of the team didn't hear him. Geoff had grabbed the good ear muffs, the rest making due with cheap gear from the student store.

"I don't think you cracked any windows," said Geoff. "And the walls seem intact, so I think we're good."

José sighed. He looked around, doing his own assessment of any possible damages. He was pretty sure his stipend didn't include building repairs. *I better tone things down*, thought José. *I can't afford to replace the whole laboratory.*

"Now, there is, of course, the matter of making amends to the rest of the lab," said Geoff. "The noise was unexpected and some of the more sensitive students don't do well with loud sounds."

José looked at Geoff in disbelief. "Amends?"

"Oh yes."

"So…donuts?" said José.

"Donuts are a good start," said Geoff. "And some of that fancy coffee from the off-campus store. I'll give you a list of what everyone likes."

"How about the Professor? What should I bring her?"

"I don't think they make coffee black enough for her taste."

Most of the lab staff had wandered off, trying to shake out the sounds ringing in their ears.

"Here," said Geoff. "Let me show you our research. I have a small version of the Proton Time Gun on my lab bench."

"Is it quiet?"

"Not really, but I've got some baffles I can use to mitigate the sound."

José looked at the device. There was not much to see. It was a black box with a funnel on one end with slots on the back for power and other connectors.

"Here, let me open it up."

Geoff undid the restraining bolts and lifted the cover, showing circuits with the usual array of capacitors, resistors and diodes.

"Interesting," said José. "No vacuum tubes, but tunable diodes, and I see some crystals. Is that to set the base signal?"

"Exactly. We pulled the crystals from old HAM rigs. There's a stack of them on a rheostat, so we can adjust the output and beat the crystals together to generate different signals."

"Where do the protons come in?" asked José.

"That's the secret sauce. It's in the box near the funnel. I can't open it. Dr. Jamieson builds them in her office workshop with no assistance. I know it sounds a little quirky, but it's her lab."

"Is it radioactive?" asked José. "I don't see a lot of shielding."

"I'm not supposed to tell anyone, but I think it has something to do with black holes or some other combination of cosmic interactions. When the Professor is building a box, we can hear the wailing of colliding atoms."

"Like a banshee wailing?" asked José.

"I guess you could call it that. It's certainly otherworldly, like something from another time and dimension."

"Do you think the military is supplying the precursors?" said José. "They have access to all sorts of weird reagents. Maybe something from Area 51?"

Geoff didn't say anything. He doubted if it was alien technology as José was implying, but he had no way to know, one way or the other.

"Tell you what," said Geoff. "If I find out, I'll let you know. Unless you want to join the Army and learn their secrets?"

José ignored the offer. The last thing he wanted to do was join an organization which had a worse reputation than high school. Most of the TimeExplorers were a little strange, and working alone in secret was their preferred methodology.

"Do you think the sounds coming out of the Proton Time Gun have anything to do with opening the TimeWall?" asked José.

"It's not designed that way, but when the crystals start banging together, it can get loud."

Geoff closed the cover and turned on the device. The room glowed with purple light as the crystals warmed up.

"Nice, so you've replaced the vacuum tubes with crystals. I should have thought of that."

Geoff replied, "They're good, but we've cracked a few trying to reach the right frequencies. Do vacuum tubes have the same problem?"

"No, the elements are isolated in the vacuum and it may protect them from cracking, or imploding, like your oscilloscopes did."

"Oh, I forgot about that. I'll have to get them replaced. I'll tell the military supplier that they were defective or something."

"It sure sounds like your studies are tightly connected with the military. Are you sure that's wise?"

"Well, they do have virtually an unlimited supply of money and Dr. Jamieson knows a few of them quite well."

"Don't tell me... She was a drill sergeant in a prior life?"

"Lt. Commander, but that wasn't a bad guess," said Geoff.

The proton gun was getting noisy, not unlike José's experiment, and without the baffles, it would require ear covering.

José thought, *That is eerily like the sounds my device produces, but much weaker.*

The device started shaking and a beam shot out, hitting the wall of the lab and dispersing a purple haze.

"I better shut it off. The university administrators don't seem to like purple beams on the other side of the wall."

"So the proton gun transmits through solids?"

Geoff nodded.

"Well, that explains why the military is interested," said José. "What else can it do besides irritate administrators?"

"That's a good point. I never thought of that option. I guess it could be tuned into a narrow beam and cause some damage."

"Let's present it to Dr. Jamieson. She might be interested," said José.

"Let's not. I'm a little afraid of our boss and her military contacts," said Geoff. "I don't want to be thrown out of the program for making a weapon."

"So, I take it you're close to completing your PhD?" asked José. "I guess I wouldn't want to rock the boat before I got into the harbor either."

Geoff's lack of an answer was a resounding yes.

Before the conversation could crash into the rocks and get the team in trouble, one of the junior grad students interrupted.

"Mr. Davidovich, Dr. Jaimeson said she wants you to present your ideas in our weekly meeting. You'll be first up tomorrow morning at 10am."

"Great," said José. "Geoff, do you have another 'scope I can borrow? I want to analyze the sounds from your Proton Time Gun."

"Still with the sounds," said Geoff. "Sure. Let me pull one from storage and you can have at it as long as you promise not to destroy it."

109

Chapter 27 -
Time to Explain

Geoff had reserved a small room for the weekly meeting. It held about thirty people auditorium style. As senior member of the team, he had the pleasure of announcing the speakers and maintaining order. The job fit his skill set to a tee.

"Dr. Jamieson, Time Lab students and guests, I'd like to present José Isaac Davidovich, our latest member of Dr. Jamieson's Time Lab."

José bowed slightly in acknowledgment.

"José is new to the program and has received the eminent 'Timeless' grant from the government's Chronology Study organization. He has some new and exciting ideas to present to the group."

"José, you're new to the group," said Geoff. "As such, I figure it would be prudent to tell you that we allow questions during the presentation in order to stimulate the conversation."

"No problem. I'm ready for anything," said José.

José had learned a lot over the years. Bus travel expanded his world and forced him to relate to other people; smart, dumb, friendly, or evil. He met people like Dr. Jamieson before and tried not to poke the bear, at least too much. He wasn't concerned about the PhD. prize but was in it for the knowledge and to drive off boredom.

"Quit the chatter," barked Dr. Jamieson. "Our newest, member of my TimeLab is going to discuss his thoughts on my Proton Time Gun. Let's see if he truly is worth the grant money."

Jose started, "Dr. Jamieson, Time Lab students, and guests. Thank you for having me present at your symposium."

José looked over the assembled group. Half a dozen TimeLab grad students, some marginally interested undergrads, a few bored professors looking for a place to zone out for a few hours and two strangers in suits who didn't seem to fit in with the rest of the group.

Those must be the Chronology Studies group, thought José. *They look like undercover officers or mafioso. I don't know which would be worse.*

"As you may have noticed from my experiment the other day, my studies revolve around sound."

Three grad students, sitting a little too close together, winced at the mention of loud sounds.

"I've been able to crack open the TimeWall by amplifying the everyday sounds leaking through Time."

Dr. Jaimeson sat up and leaned over to Geoff. He shook his head.

"What in blue blazes is he talking about?" she whispered. "Doesn't he know that my Proton Time Gun is the only way to break through the TimeWall?"

"I'm sure he'll get to that," said Geoff. "This is just the preamble to get everyone's attention."

"He better," whispered Dr. Jaimeson. "The military is here and I don't want them to get the wrong idea. Funding depends on having a unified message."

"Let's give him a chance to explain," said Geoff. "I'm sure he will come around to support your position."

"If he doesn't he's out of the program."

José waited for the background chatter to die down and continued.

"I'm sure you've all heard the soft banshee sounds by now," said José.

One of the bolder grad students raised a hand, "Do you mean the tinnitus? My grandfather has that, it drives him crazy."

"I've seen your granddad," whispered another student. "If that's the reason for his actions, I'm not ready to get old."

"No," replied the first student. "That's the drinking."

José answered the implied questions. "No. The banshee sounds are completely different. You have to be very quiet to hear them. They're not constant, but in the right circumstances they can be clearly heard."

Geoff was ready to interrupt but thought better. *I'll let him hoist himself on his own petard. It's not my job to convince him differently.*

José thought, *This may be a tough audience. My* tio *never has a problem with my theories, but Time studies is not his main source of research.*

"I was able to sample the soft sounds coming through the TimeWall. I've always felt that these were banshee-like, the sad chatter of TimeWorld, the audible protests of life passing away as time moved on."

"That's a little creepy," whispered another grad student.

Dr. Jaimeson leaned over to Geoff, "Have we ever tried to hear those sounds?"

"After his little stunt with the oscilloscopes, no one in the lab can hear much of anything," said Geoff.

"That reminds me. I'm going to take the associated cost out of his stipend. We can't have students going around recklessly destroying lab equipment, now can we?"

José continued, ignoring the buzz of dissension. "I was able to isolate the sound frequencies and focus the amplitude to activate the QTmBits surrounding the TimeWall."

A snort of derision, not from Dr. Jaimeson, could be heard from one of the grad students.

Dr. Jaimeson smiled. *I taught my students well. They're not believing this claptrap any more than I am.*

"Okay. You're going to have to explain that term," said Dr. Jamieson.

"Sorry, I probably should have made a PowerPoint," said José.

There was a universal groan from the audience.

"That's okay," said Geoff. "We typically don't use those types of presentations."

"Anyhow," José continued. "The QTmBits connect all the Shadows behind the TimeWall, keeping the slices together as you move in the Now."

"And how do you know this?" asked Geoff.

"I thought that was obvious," said José. "I saw them when I cracked the TimeWall a few years ago."

Dr. Jamieson leaned back and turned to the suits and said, "He's a new student and we allow them to express themselves. Everyone knows the Proton Time Gun is the only viable solution."

The suits nodded, showing no emotion. The poker face of undercover agents.

Geoff asked, "So, you can replicate your work? We'd like to see your equipment."

"I'm working on it," said José. "My machine was destroyed after my last journey beyond the TimeWall. Replacement parts are hard to find. I was hoping to expand the research here in the TimeLab."

"We'll see," Dr. Jaimeson grunted.

Geoff knew an exit song when he heard one. "Thank you, José. Your talk has been quite enlightening. We look forward to seeing your machine in action, as well as this TimeWall you mentioned."

"Okay, everyone, it looks like we still have plenty of work ahead of us," said Dr. Jamieson. "The military has funded the research for another year and they're looking for results. I'll be in my office and don't wish to be disturbed. Geoff, please join me after I talk with our esteemed guests."

The two suits and Dr. Jamieson adjourned to her office for a quick conversation.

Dr. Jamieson started the discussion. "I must apologize for the new student's less-than-stellar seminar. He came highly recommended from one of the professors and scored very high on the aptitude tests."

Suit Number One said, "No apology needed. The government appreciates innovation and new thinking."

Suit Number Two replied, "Of course, all the funding is tied to the Proton Gun. There is no line-item for sound exploration."

"It shouldn't be a problem. He is on a small stipend, barely a pittance. If he starts infecting the other students with his weird ideas or inhibits the project, I'll pull his funds and toss him out on his ear."

The three parted company and Geoff entered the office.

Dr. Jaimeson spoke quietly, "Geoff, you better do something about the new student. I don't want him tossing his crazy ideas around. The military threatened to kill the project if it went in a different direction. They are committed to the Proton Gun."

"Understood, Professor," said Geoff. "I'll let him down easy. I want to see what he knows and use the information for the Proton Time Gun. If that's alright with you."

"Do what you must. Tell him the stipend has been withdrawn and he must be out by the end of the semester. That should give you time to quiz the poor deluded fool."

"Consider it done, Professor."

Chapter 28 -
Time for a Bulldozer

José left the university after losing his stipend, and Dr. Jaimeson's group kept trying to find a break in Time. Dr. Jaimeson continued working with her students, getting nowhere while while burning up funds and irritating the administrators with her purple beams and noise. The project picked up steam after the video of José's TimeWall escapade made its rounds. The government was able to suppress the information for the most part, and money poured into the Time Lab to duplicate his success.

Dr. Jaimeson and her crew of grad students returned to the area where the TimeWall was found and continued looking for a signal indicating a break in Time. Geoff walked over to where Professor Jamieson was sitting on a folding chair, overseeing the student-led random search. Geoff, as senior grad student, had the unenviable job of bringing bad news to his mercurial major professor.

"Dr. Jamieson, we've tried every sensor and checked every blade of grass," said Geoff. "And there are no signs of a crack in the TimeWall or remnants of the Time Explorer."

"Don't call that reprobate an explorer!" said Dr. Jamieson. "No random person can duplicate what I've done with my Proton Time Gun machine. I'm sure he's broken into my lab and stolen my designs."

"We have no record of a break-in," said Geoff. "I've reviewed all the logs. Nothing is missing."

Dr. Jamieson thought, *Maybe the grad students are turning against me? I'll check with my military contacts, they can help. I don't trust Jeff. He can't even spell his name correctly.*

Dr. Jamieson looked around the search area and said, "I think we'll set up a branch lab here. The university administrators are leery of the Proton Time Gun. The fools think it could damage their exquisite old buildings. I mean, just because a building is old doesn't mean it's special. You watch, once we break through the TimeWall we'll be able to change the future. Maybe I'll build them a better building."

"Yes, Professor," said Geoff, using his correct spelling.

"Jeff, I want you to find out who owns this piece of dirt. We need to build a testing lab on the site. It's isolated and away from the controlling university administration."

"Yes, Professor. I'll get right on it. Do you have a plan for the lab?"

"I don't know," said Dr. Jamieson. "Tell them we need to bulldoze the knoll, add parking and access for large trucks. I'm sure I can get the military to give me a Quonset hut we can use for the work."

"How big will the building be?"

"How the hell would I know! I'm not a construction engineer, Use the standard size. You're a grad student, don't you know how to look things up?"

One of the other grad students furiously typed on their cell phone and presented the findings to Geoff.

"Yes, Professor," said Geoff. "I checked and a twenty by forty-eight foot hut would fit in this area. I'll contact the county building department and get the permits started."

"That's too small. I want one twice that size. And don't waste your time getting permits," said the Professor. "I'll have my military contacts run interference should any city official decide to stick their nose in places it doesn't belong. They're paying for it. There's money in my budget and they will do anything to get access to the past. I want this new lab up and running within six months."

"Yes, Professor," said Geoff. "I do have one question. Does it have to be a Quonset Hut? I'm sure there are funds to build a modern lab."

"Grad students don't make decisions. Don't forget that. A Quonset Hut is what we're getting. Anyhow, it reminds me of my military days. Those were fun."

Dr. Jaimeson reached down for her bullhorn and yelled. "Everyone stop working and come over here!"

The students surrounded their boss, keeping well out of any danger zone in case their professor exploded. Dr. Jamieson started giving orders. "Listen up. I'm only going to say this once. We're going to set up a testing lab on this site. Jeff will be in charge."

"It's Geoff, not Jeff," said Geoff.

Dr. Jamieson gave a withering glance at her star student and said, "As I was saying, Jeff will be in charge. I want to see a show of hands of anyone who has construction experience."

The students were hesitant to reply. They went to the university because they didn't want to get their hands dirty, and now it looked like they would become nothing more than underpaid construction workers.

One of the students slowly raised her hand. "I helped my father assemble a shed once."

"That's it? No one else?"

As in any line of unwilling draftees, no one else responded.

"Fine, you'll be Jeff's assistant. What's your name?"

The student stammered.

"Never mind. Jeff and what's-her-name will be in charge. The rest of you, start learning skills that require shovels and picks. You'll have to purchase your own hard hats, the military doesn't have a clothing allowance in the grants and I'm not made of money."

The students were stuck. They wanted their PhD's and the job description implied that they would do anything their boss wanted. While they would deny it in public, they would help bury a body if it meant success in their chosen field.

The narrow mountain road had to suffer the indignity of large trucks compressing its thin topping of cheap asphalt.

The bulldozers and scrapers made short work of the knoll. Who knew what apparition left over from José's travel was unceremoniously displaced in the process?

A line of concrete trucks struggled up the hill, dropping their gray cement to seal the lab from living dirt. The lab, balanced on cement and surrounded by vibrant foothills, stood like a wart on the green earth.

Geoff was in his element. Back at the university, he ordered everyone to pack up the proton gun and its prototypes as the military hauled in an old Quonset hut on the newly prepped location. The back door faced the foothills, ready to blast a hole in Time.

It took a year, even with Dr. Jamieson cracking the whip. She could make her students work faster, but they knew nothing about construction. The contractors and their workers ignored the students. They weren't even in the same union.

Testing on the proton gun proceeded back at the university. It still didn't work, but everyone at the school was happy to hear that the Time Study group would soon have a home. Aside from the noise factor, many of the faculty and students were worried that a tiny nuclear reactor was used to generate the protons for each shot.

While the fast elements didn't cause any destruction, as such, no one knew where the errant protons went during testing. Being downwind from the Time Lab was considered bad placement and reserved for junior staff. Fortunately, the lab faced the sports stadium and the over-trained athletes probably thought proton irradiation was an asset. Their win/loss records seemed to disagree.

Moving day came none too soon. The job of overseeing the move and new lab facilities aged Geoff. Dr. Jaimeson did not age well either. She resorted to a cane and hobbled around with the excess weight of age and tired joints. The cane made her more intimidating. Now everyone had to keep out of striking distance if they contradicted her theories.

Chapter 29 -
Time for a Proton

José fired up the TimeWall device in his basement lab. It was working again, but it only generated a small break in the TimeWall. He was able to slide a fiber-optic cable through, but it showed a gray swirling mist with no detail.

José turned to Paquito, half-asleep still wearing his ear protection. Paquito lifted up his head as the banshee screams became a human voice.

"I sort of miss my *madre* banging on the floor, trying to get me to shut my 'toy' off." Jose grabbed the countertop then slowly sat down as thoughts of Spam™ burritos and his mother intruded.

"You miss her too, don't you, Paquito?"

The chihuahua, old but not deaf, nodded and went back to sleep.

"This better not be my Shadows sneaking through the gap and messing with my mind. Oh well, nothing I can do about that now. Maybe if my Shadows are up to it, I can ask them to check up on her."

"I'm sure my gear is functioning, unless there is something subtly different with the old hardware? Everything checks out, but something is missing. I know the vacuum tubes were not the exact part number as the original set, but they're close enough."

José grabbed a multimeter probe, looking for an electronic solution.

"I wonder if TimeWall access is location dependent?"

Before José went on a road trip to find specific rare parts, he knew what he had to do to test the equipment. He boosted the volume until the rock wall foundation started cracking, fine mortar dust filling the air. The TimeWall was bubbling, pushing out toward José, but still no larger than a silver dollar.

A car drove by, honking, answering the call of the sirens.

"I better shut it down. I think the neighbors might not care for my experiments."

"One more thing I can check, I'll go back to the knoll below the foothills and see if that makes a difference."

The next morning, José prepared by loading his bicycle into the back seat of his mother's car, then puttered around the house getting ready.

"I better make a sandwich, it'll be a full day, I'm sure. Cookies would be nice, too."

José approached the designated spot. "What's this? I don't remember that road. It looks like someone bulldozed it through 'lovers lane'."

He drove up to the next turnout and unloaded his gear.

"I better take a side path. Who knows what else is up there?"

Stealth was important and pushing his bike and gear was never going to be pleasant, but riding could be tricky on the seldom-used paths and he didn't want to crash. A high fence topped with barbed wire blocked his path.

"Darn, there are buildings on my old stomping grounds. No way I'm getting in there. Maybe I'll just go around, or maybe there is a break I can find."

He spotted a placard hanging on the wire fence.

Dr. Jamieson, Time Professor
Memorial Time Laboratory
Restricted area by order of the University
Sponsored by the U.S. Army.

———

**All civilians must
check in at the guard station
before proceeding.**

———

That doesn't look good, thought José. *Maybe they had the same idea and the TimeWall entrance must be location-specific.*

He snuck around the facility keeping to a low spot in the rising foothills. Squeaky springs announced a rising garage door on the Quonset hut facing the knoll.

"Of course," said José, "That must be where they keep the proton time device. Look at the size of that beast. I bet there's a nuclear reactor nearby to power the monster."

The proton gun was funnel-shaped with the stem attached to a car-sized box.

José had questions, "I wonder what that must do to the TimeWall? It doesn't look portable. Do they have to drive it through the wall to reopen it on the other side? Maybe they have it on a timer?"

As José sat, pondering the device and trying to make sense of his questions. The ground started shaking as eerie sounds beat the air. A purple energy stream shot out of the funnel, bouncing off the bubbles making up the now visible TimeWall.

"Interesting," said José, "The sounds are just like my time box. I bet the lights are just for show, I'm sure the sounds are bringing up the wall."

The black box started smoking and a burst of sound and light highlighted the weak, ribbon-like wall. Dr. Jamieson's Memorial Proton Time Gun, burped out a purple blast of steam and shut down.

"What do you know? I guess they still can't get it working. If that is all they have, I doubt they even understand the process."

Technicians came scurrying out of the garage, looking busy and scared. An older, heavy-set woman followed the techs, walking stiffly with the aid of a cane. The techs appeared to be trying to keep out of the way of the looming presence and her cane.

Wait a minute, isn't that Dr. Jamieson, herself? thought José. *I thought you had to be dead to be memorialized. I guess if you're mean enough you can get most anything.*

He strained to hear what was going on, but action spoke as loud as words. It looked like they were getting ready for another test.

Dr. Jamieson looked at her precious proton gun. "What have you done? Why is it steaming? Did anyone see the TimeWall? I'm sure it appeared."

Geoff, now a professor in the TimeLab had the unenviable job of keeping the good Doctor happy and running interference for the rest of the crew.

"It's just a minor glitch, Professor," said Geoff. "We've almost got the beam tuned up. I'm sure it will work on the next attempt."

"It better," huffed Dr. Jamieson. "We have an inspection later this week and we don't want to disappoint the military."

"Yes, Professor," said Geoff. "We'll have it up and running by the time the brass shows up."

"You better or you can kiss your PhD goodbye," said Dr. Jaimeson.

Geoff didn't say anything; this was the Professor's go-to response to anything that didn't go her way, including scientific findings. By his count he had already lost nine PhD's over the last couple of years.

"You, over there, in the blue smock," shouted Dr. Jamieson. "Yes you, the tech with the glasses. I want you to check every bolt and wiring harness. I'm sure I heard a loose wire sputter before the Proton Time Gun failed."

"I'll make sure they do the work correctly," said Geoff. "Why don't you step inside the nice, cool lab and get a cup of tea?"

Dr. Jaimeson turned red, "I'm not some doddering old fool. I can destroy your career at the drop of a hat."

Geoff didn't say anything.

"Now get out of my way. I'll be in my office and expect you to fix this immediately."

"Of course, Professor," said Geoff.

The doctor hobbled into the lab proper, sat in her chair, and sighed, "This project will be the death of me. If we didn't have evidence from that strange man years ago, I would have given this up for a nice position, teaching elemental Time theory at the Junior college."

Fortunately, no one was nearby to record the threat/offer. Geoff turned to one of the newer grad students and said, "Please get a pot of tea for the professor, something soothing, with a shot of whiskey."

Chapter 30 -
Time for Geoff

José ducked out of view of the laboratory staff and laid his bike nearby.

"It looks like Dr. Jamieson hasn't lost a beat over the years. Sure glad I'm not in that program anymore."

"What can I do? There's no way I can use my backpack time device here. Everyone would know as soon as I fired it up and the banshee screaming starts."

At the proton garage, Dr Jamieson was done drinking her calming tea and came out to the front end of the Proton Time Gun, peering in its barrel and brandishing her cane, pointing out everything she thought needed adjustment.

"I know what to do. I can piggyback on their gun. They won't notice my noise and I bet they are too frightened of their boss to look around'.

"I'm a little tired, I'll just hang out here behind the hilltop and enjoy the nice weather while they work on their Proton Time Gun."

The proton team reassembled their gun in record time and once the concert started, José woke up from his nap. His noisy Time breaker took a moment to fire up and could hardly be heard against the sounds of the Proton Time Gun echoing across the foothills. The TimeWall shimmered into existence and José could hear cheers from the proton team. "So, the TimeWall is location dependent! It sounds as if the proton gun is piggybacked on my generator instead. Wait until they try to replicate their experiment without my help."

With that, José stepped through the TimeWall into his familiar time world. The first thing he saw was his replicant, with an angry face.

>There you are! Do you know what's been going on here?

"Of course not. I just got here. Are you telling me everything isn't fun and peaceful behind the Now?

>No, just look around. Your Time friends have been wreaking havoc on our world.

José noticed that Shadows linked to the Now were rough around the edges and the QTmBit strings were thin, barely holding on. On top of the weakened links, some of the trees, grasses and the nearby environment were no longer connected to their source-hosts beyond the TimeWall.

>Why did you come back to this location? We were happy at your laboratory.

"Well, I couldn't get the TimeWall to expand. It only seems to work here."

>So what? We could see you. Isn't that enough?

"No. I don't want the TimeWall to be a one-way device with me on the outside. But at least I figured out the solution. I guess there are a limited number of locations for a good connection."

Faces flipped, and not for the best.

>Fine. The scientist discovered something. Now do something about your friends. They're destroying our world with their high-energy blasts.

"Sorry, they're not my friends, but let's go over and check them out. If I ask nicely, I'm sure they'll be willing to help."

>No. We don't care about your friends and we don't want to go with you.

"Fine, I'll go, you stay."

>You know that's not how it works. Where you go we follow.

José walked toward the proton gun. He saw a string of replica guns inside a Quonset hut receding off into the distance. Shadows milled about, slipping through each other as the students in the Now ran around checking on the device. None of the students or techs crossed in front of the gun, with its purple shimmering electronic blast.

"I sure hope that thing doesn't blow up. Would it cause a permanent hole in Time or blow away my Shadows once and for all?"

>We heard that. Let's get out of here.

"It was only me thinking out loud. I saw a prototype of the Proton Time Gun, remember? You were there, too. I'm sure there won't be any explosions."

At least I hope there aren't, thought José

>You better be careful, once you get back to the Now, we'll check with your newest Shadow and see what you really think.

"And do what? You have no power over the Now."

Faces flipped, looking for the right face. Threats were never José's forte, and it took a while for the attitude to show up.

>That you know of.

José dismissed the empty threats and checked out what was happening with Dr. Jaimeson's experiment. Shadows of action filled the space behind Time, a frantic crisscross of moving lines.

"Are they going to send out a robot or just stick some probes through the TimeWall? I bet they get no signal on their end. I've never been able to take anything back from behind the Now, no matter what I've tried."

His Shadows waved and pointed to the center of the purple stream. There was one person on his side of the TimeWall, dressed in a white hazmat suit complete with a re-breather connected by an umbilical cord through the wall. The hazmat person raised their hand and a muffled voice came out.

"Greetings TimePerson. I'm Geoff, and I bring tidings from the other side of time. I'm part of Dr. Jamieson's Time experiments. We come in peace."

It took all of José's self-control not to laugh.

"Geoff. Welcome to Time. I am its master. Bow to me or be consumed by my horde of time Shadows."

José's Shadows got in on the joke and started moving toward Geoff, ready to surround him.

Geoff dropped to his knees. "Forgive the intrusion, TimeMaster. I'm only a poor student trying to learn about your realm."

"Stand, Sir Geoff, and take off that silly mask. It's me, José. We met at the Timeless BBQ years ago."

"Timeless BBQ?" Geoff did as instructed. "What do you mean? How could we have met? Do you mean that this isn't your kingdom?"

"No, Geoff, there are no kingdoms behind the TimeWall, at least none that I'm aware of," said José. "I'm just another TimeExplorer like you. I think your proton gun only worked because I turned on my sound generator, and your gun picked up on the signal."

Geoff's most recent string of Shadows reflected his actions as he got ready for the journey beyond the Now. Shadows got smaller as Time continued on its journey to its end.

"Look around, Geoff. There is your past."

Geoff's Shadows waved, and Geoff sank to his knees, again, trembling.

Each of the most recent Shadows had to deal with the re-breather. Later Shadows had Geoff's face in all its replications.

"Wait," said Geoff. "You mean the Proton Time Gun doesn't work?"

"It didn't work when I was a student in the Professor's lab, and it still doesn't work," said José.

127

"Oh my. Dr. Jamieson won't be happy. Not to mention the military."

"Not my problem. I won't tell if you won't."

"But they're recording everything. They'll know by now."

"Funny thing about the TimeWall. As far as I can tell, it wipes all the data when it is passed back to the Now. They, like me, will have no record of what happens here."

"That's horrible," said Geoff. "If there is no data shown, the project is worthless."

Geoff sank to his knees again "This will hurt my chance of getting tenure. I can't work anywhere else. The university is all I know."

"I suppose, if that is important to you."

"Can I meet with you? Will you be my mentor? Where do you live?"

Before José could answer the plea, the proton gun flashed a deep red color, and Geoff was unceremoniously yanked back to the other side of Time.

Chapter 31 -
Time to Debrief

Purple gas enveloped Geoff as he popped back from the other side of Time, looking like an oversized fairy without wings.

"What happened?" shouted Dr. Jamieson. "Did you see the past?"

"There was nothing but a gray, smelly fog," replied Geoff.

"You took off the mask to check out the air?" admonished Dr. Jamieson. "That's a serious breach in protocol. I could rescind your PhD for that."

"It was fine. I had a feeling there was no danger. I was able to breathe, and we need to know if that is possible."

"That was supposed to happen after we sampled the air and ran it through the MassSpec in phase three of the study. Here I thought you were one of my best students."

"It was fine," said Geoff. "Just gray and smelly."

Dr. Jaimeson muttered, "I'm going to have to reconsider letting Jeff get tenure. I don't need another loose cannon running around."

Dr. Jaimeson turned to one of the other grad students. "We need to get him checked for viruses and bacteria."

"Do we need an ambulance?" asked the student.

"No. I'll get my military contact to take care of it. We can put Jeff in isolation. For as long as it takes."

She turned to Geoff. "Put your mask back on. Stay in the suit until we get you cleared."

"Well, now you can skip that step," said Geoff. "I'm fine. There was nothing beyond the Now. Everything's gone."

"I can't accept that answer," said Dr. Jamieson. "We need to go back. I'll check myself. It'll be easy now that we know how to open the TimeWall."

Geoff looked down, not wanting to tell Dr. Jamieson that the Proton Time Gun may not work without the missing sound component.

"The military might disapprove of you running around after breathing unfiltered past air," said Dr. Jamieson. "But I won't bring it up, this time. You're on thin ice, mister."

Dr. Jamieson was the Queen of empty threats. She needed Geoff as much as he needed a job at the university. They were at mutual-destruction lying levels.

"Are you sure you didn't see anything?" said Dr. Jamieson.

Dr. Jamieson's military background started to kick in, and she thought, *I don't believe him. Do I have to waterboard Jeff to get a straight answer? Maybe I'll do that anyway for breaking protocol. It might be fun.*

"There's nothing but fog."

"Nothing moving? No shadows? No echo of the Now?"

Geoff sighed. *Does she know about the Shadows? She's been studying Time forever. Will she renege my tenure if I don't tell the truth?*

Dr. Jamieson's years in military intelligence recognized Geoff's hidden language and said, "Ah ha! You did find out something else. Confess before I get mad."

For most people, the thought of someone being mad at you was a minor risk. It was only words. Geoff had worked with Dr. Jamieson since he first entered the graduate program and he knew an empty threat when he heard one. This one was not empty. Dr. Jamieson's threat could mean the end of his career or worse.

"Okay, there were one-dimensional shadows of everything in the Now, stretching off into the distant past."

"I knew it. Just like my earlier experiments, before I added the Proton Time Gun to the sound array."

Geoff thought, *Of course there were earlier experiments! The Proton Gun design came after the military started to fund the project. Dr. Jamieson just added bling to the project to sell it to the Army.*

"Why did you call them Shadows? We've never talked about them in any class I taught."

"It seemed to be the right name; they were gray and thin, so a Shadow."

"What else? Any animals or other unusual beings?"

130

Geoff was beyond worried. Lying to someone who may have been an intelligent officer was not good for one's career or health.

"Just one. José."

"What's a José? Is that some sort of cryptid? I know there are monsters behind the TimeWall, I can just feel it."

"I don't know about that. All I saw was a guy with a backpack and a red bicycle. He told me to take off my mask. He seemed to be human and we talked a bit."

"Did he mention where he lived or how we could find him? I'd like to talk with him, and I know some of the military crew would be interested in finding out what he did to break through the TimeWall."

"I was pulled back before I could get his address, but we had met at the Timeless BBQ a few years ago."

"You broke bread with those malcontents? I told everyone not to go to those meetings. Your tenure may be at risk, buddy."

"The military was there, too."

"Good, at least they made sure you didn't get into any trouble. You didn't tell these weirdos about my work, did you?"

"Of course not," said Geoff. "I did sign the Non-Disclosure Agreement. I'd never mention the details of the project."

Geoff was going to avoid water torture, for now. But he had a lot of explaining to do. Being careful with words was a skill he learned after working with Dr. Jamieson over the years.

On the other side of the TimeWall, José saw Professor Jamieson and Geoff having an animated discussion.

"I knew I should have learned how to read lips. I'd love to hear this discussion."

José turned away from the echo of the Now and faced his Shadows, "Hey me's. Can you get to their Shadows and listen in?"

>Not easily. How come you keep on asking us to do new things? We were happy with you on the other side of the wall, quietly failing."

"That's a little rude. The absence of success isn't failing. Learning what doesn't work is as important as success."

131

>Said the host who spent years trying to visit us and failing.

"Aren't you lucky that I can now join you anytime I want? I'm giving you a chance to grow and learn. You don't want to be static all your existence, do you?"

> We are static. We like it like that. It's hard enough for us to follow you from behind, without having to do your bidding. We don't like spying on other Shadows.

One of the distant Shadows waved and said,

>>I'll do it. I like to spy on things.

José thought, *I don't remember that personality. I wonder what I was thinking back then.*

The lead Shadow spoke for the line.

>But we don't have any say in this, do we?"

"Exactly. Spill what you know."

>Shadows don't usually share with other Shadows unless they know you well in the Now.

"Perfect. I know both of the parties, sneak in there and give me a report."

>It's not that easy. Geoff knows about Shadows and we should be able to communicate. Dr. Jamieson, probably not. Remember your earlier contact with her? We chatted with her Shadows then, and they threatened violence if we ever came back. A shadow can't easily forget.

"Yes. I remember that short stint in her lab. We never did agree on the concepts or how the experiments should be run. I think she got my funding cut off, but I could never prove it."

On the other side of Time, Geoff gesticulated in José's general direction while Dr. Jamieson waved her cane around in a threatening manner.

"Oh, this is too good. I really need to find out what's going on. I'd do most anything to be able to listen in."

>Like activate your boom-box and step into their Now?

"Anything but that. No way I'm going to share my findings until I'm ready."

>We figured that out already.

"Maybe I can open a small window and listen in.

>Risky, don't expect us to help.

132

"I'm going to do it. All I should have to do is de-tune the vacuum tubes and force a small hole open."

>We're not responsible for what happens. Don't do it!

"Of course you're not responsible. I am. I'm the host."

Geoff and Dr. Jamieson stopped their lively discussion as a dime-sized TimeWall appeared near the Proton Time Gun.

"Do you see that?" said Geoff. "I'm sure that's the TimeExplorer trying to contact me."

"The José? That's impossible. Where would it get enough power to run a Proton Time Gun?"

"That's what I've been trying to tell you. He doesn't have a proton gun, just a backpack and a bike."

José strained to hear the conversation, but it sounded just like the gray background noise filling all of TimeWorld.

"I guess he'll never know. I might as well go back and step out of Time. Now that I know the parameters, it will be easy to come back."

>Please don't open the wall here. What if they try to run the Proton Time Gun?

The TimeWall flashed red as the sun. Earth turned and sunset began.

"It's been a long day. I can come back later. I promised my *madre* to return the car with a full tank of gas and I don't want to drive the windy road at night in that old car"

Chapter 32 -
Time for a Job

José made it back before nightfall with an almost full tank of gas and an empty stomach.

"I need to pack more food for the next trip. Dealing with my Shadows takes a lot of energy. I'll ask my *madre* to make a few burritos for the road. At least I don't have to share them with my Shadows. I wonder how they make it without food? I'll have to ask them how that works."

He set his equipment on the workbench and his bike against the wall.

"The vacuum tubes were sputtering. I should replace them and check on the capacitors, they're starting to overheat. The last thing I want is to be stuck on the wrong side of the wall with those *meshuggeneh* Shadows."

His Shadows couldn't be seen or heard, but they kept track of their host.

>Is he insulting us again? Who here knows Yiddish?

A shadow way back in the line waved and said

>>>>I do. It means crazy. I don't think it's being used in a nice way.

>What's wrong with his side of Time? We haven't hurt him lately.

>>I'm sure he meant no offense. Anyhow, if he stays with us too long, he'd probably starve to death.

>You're right. I hope he brings better food next time. I don't like the constant tuna-fish sandwiches.

>>What difference does it make? We can't eat anything he brings.

>It's the thought that counts. He should be more considerate of our well-being.

>>Great. Send him a message. I'm sure that would work.

>Okay. I'll be quiet, like a good Shadow.

With no job and blackballed from graduate school, José had time on his hands and he began rebuilding his Time machine. He was quite happy to decipher dying noises sneaking through the TimeWall instead of working on a meaningless higher degree. As much as he listened, no banshees talked to him and the Shadows didn't influence him. And he still liked tuna-fish sandwiches.

"I feel sorry for Geoff. It looked like he was being put through the wringer after our little talk behind the TimeWall. I probably shouldn't have reminded him about the Timeless BBQ. At least he doesn't know where I live."

Carlos was in the kitchen visiting his sister-in-law while José kept to his workshop laboratory. Fresh coffee and discussions revolved around the current world situation, TV shows, and what José was going to do with his future. By convention, talk about José's papa was not part of the conversation.

"I'm worried about the boy," said Lara. "He doesn't seem to have any direction. The noise coming from the basement is getting on my nerves."

"It could be worse," said Carlos. "He's not in a gang and doesn't seem to be taking drugs."

"Not having those traits is a pretty low bar," said Lara. "I was hoping that he would complete a university degree and maybe get a job as a professor, like you did."

"Teaching is not everything it's cracked up to be," replied Carlos. "The university system can be brutal. It's usually hidden behind a facade of intellectualism, but the knives come out for anyone who doesn't fit into the system. Leaving the university might have been for the best."

"It seems to have worked out well for you," said Lara. "Maybe you can get him back in as an assistant or something?"

"That would be tricky. University gossip is pervasive. If the professor who kicked him out hears of it, there would be hell to pay. She is quite powerful."

"That may be, but the university is better than tinkering. You can't make a living playing with electronic toys."

"You're right," said Carlos. "Everything is throw-away now. There's no future in repairing things. I have some contacts outside of the university. There's a new business opening up and José's tinkering might be what they need."

José wasn't privy to the family planning commission, but he felt that he may have worn out his welcome in the basement and considered hitting the road again.

And worse, he couldn't get the time-breaking devices to work no matter how he fiddled with the setup.

"I should have hoarded more pieces at the Timeless BBQ swap table," said José. "I could have given a power supply or rheostat instead of my limited stock of vacuum tubes. It's not as if anyone gave me credit for my gift. Vacuum tubes are just about impossible to find now that RadioShack® has gone out of business. I can barely find any worthwhile electronics at the local shops. I hope I can get it back working."

Unfortunately, taking TimeWall electronics back to bare metal and rebuilding is always more difficult than expected. For now, he had nothing but parts lying around and had no idea how long it would take to get his machine back to working order.

He wandered upstairs for a cup of coffee. Something hot and caffeinated is what he needed to get the ideas moving.

"José," said his *tio*. "Your mother is worried about your future without a solid job."

"I'm doing fine, *Tio*," said José. "I've got a few repair jobs lined up. You don't have to worry I can always find odd jobs when I need money."

"Nevertheless, we both think you should find some steady work. I have an offer for you."

José knew that his mother and his *tio* had the best intentions for him and his future and didn't say anything as Carlos talked.

"We know you love fixing things," said Carlos. "And there is a new company starting up that can use your skills."

"*Gracias, Tio* Carlos. I guess I could give it a try. I know I can't depend on you and my *madre* to support me. I'm willing to try it, if it will help my *madre* out."

"That's my boy," said Carlos. "I'm sure you can do well. A regular job will be a nice change."

His mother sighed. "I'll pack lunches so you can save money."

José was given a bench at an up-and-coming company and proved himself invaluable. They wisely sent him company-wide as a troubleshooter and ignored the weird noises emanating from his cubicle.

Chapter 33 -
Time for NightLite

José joined the new employees for orientation; it was the usual lectures on the history of the founders, their vision for their business, warnings about the dangers of the high-powered equipment and sexual/harassment classes. José sat in the back of the auditorium paying just enough attention to pass the multiple-choice tests at the end of the sessions. His seatmate was a young man with a short haircut and pallid complexion.

"Hi. I'm Danton. I was hired as a junior engineer. What are you in here for?"

"José," said José. "And nothing as fancy as that. I'm more of a fix-it person."

"That's good to know. What's your expertise?"

"I can fix most anything. Electronics, computers, woodworking, I can even do a bit of welding if needed. I tinker with Time, too."

"Those are impressive skills, as long as you have time to do the work."

The fishing expedition for fellow Time enthusiasts didn't even get a bite, but there were lots of other engineers, and he should be able to find someone with similar interests. Not that he needed help devising his Time machine, but the engineers were skilled at looking at a problem and coming up with unique solutions.

José was given a bench and a smock and quickly proved himself invaluable. His immediate supervisors wisely sent him company-wide as a skilled fixer and ignored the weird noises emanating from his cubicle. He seemed to be able to fix anything from wonky electronics to misbehaving desks. The only thing he wouldn't work on was plumbing. Not from lack of ability but having too much sense to risk an unwanted shower or worse. He left that to the professionals.

Most of the engineers focused on gaining experience to move up the corporate ladder and were not interested in anything not directly connected to their job. That was fine with José. He enjoyed repairing things and would rather be on call instead of being stuck in one place all day.

In his cubicle he displayed pictures of his *madre* and his papa when they were younger. The rest of the photos were of *Tio* Carlos and his kids. He didn't include his *tio*'s wife, since he never knew when his *tio* would find another true love of his life.

His cubicle became his own private space. He had a whiteboard where he could make notes on his Time theories and a cassette tape of Georgian chants and Banshee singing. The rest of the room was filled with tools and half-repaired instruments. It was the type of OCD chaos that he preferred.

José mentioned his Time theories to a few of the engineers, but no one was especially interested in discussing weird physics with a simple maintenance worker.

He had a few work acquaintances who were on nodding levels, but no one was interested in Time theories as much as he was. Most only watched Time's flow to determine how long it would be until they could retire. José wasn't shy about his taste in music; Matching up ancient banshee wailing with Gregorian chants was a special type of sound shielding.

Half the employees hated what he passed off as an interesting musical hobby. There were a few complaints over the years, but singing was considered innocuous compared to the other shenanigans high-ranking officers seemed to get themselves into on a regular basis.

The rest, mostly introverted engineers, thought it was a brilliant idea, a way to keep people away so they could work in peace. The only downside for them was that there was a limited selection of music that could drive neighbors away and not cause pain to the listener.

The realities of working for a living and taking care of his mother and the house left little time to work on the experiments. Writing concepts on the board was something he could explore when work wasn't pressing, but that wasn't the same as firing up his TimeWall device. He didn't stop working on his life's project completely; if nothing else, he could spend nights sorting through and testing his collection of old vacuum tubes looking for ones that would support his dreams.

The junior engineers and lowly maintenance crew were called into a meeting to discuss investment opportunities that were recently approved.

At the front of the room was someone dressed as a salesperson. A blue blazer over a pleated dress with smart, low heel shoes. The meeting started off with a condescending introduction followed by an almost endless supply of PowerPoint slides filled with meaningless charts and graphs.

"Most of you have already signed up to put part of your salary into the company's retirement funds. I congratulate you on your forward thinking. As you can see in this slide, the company has recently approved matching funds for anyone who meets the minimum requirements."

His buddy Danton sat next to José and said. "That looks impressive, but I have a new kid. I need every penny of my salary, and then some."

"I might take them up on the offer," said José. "My expenses are low, since I'm living in my *madre's* home. My only costs are for gas and food."

"Must be nice," said Danton. "My kids take a lot of money to keep them in tennis shoes and jeans. I don't know what I'll do when they grow up and want to start dating."

José nodded. Listening to his friend complain was better than paying attention to the salesperson drone on and on.

"I don't even know what I'll do about college. I wonder if they would want to go to tech schools."

"I think I'll sign up for the max amount," said José. "It sounds like I can get medical coverage too for not much more money."

"Don't get me wrong, I love my kids, but that may have to wait until I get a promotion. It takes all I have to stay even. I'll keep to the lower tier and let the future decide for itself. Won't the kids be surprised when they find out they have to support me in my old age?"

José signed the paperwork, knowing that his future was safe as long as he worked at the company long enough to get vested.

The nascent Internet of the day became José's friend, helping him find unusual electronic pieces on the swap boards. The dark web may have crept into his computer for some of the more obscure pieces. The source of his equipment was a minor issue for José since that was where the most unique pieces could be found. As every year passed, more precise and interesting hardware made it from distant warehouses and junk collections to his basement lab.

"I should drop by Tom's shop. I have time off I have to take. We cleared out all the gear, the last time I was there, but he might have a source for additional equipment. I'll try to go on my next vacation. I hope he's still there."

Chapter 34-
Time Passes

The basement was getting filled up with boxes of supplies. José insisted he wasn't a hoarder, but rather a collector of old electronics. It could have been a museum, without visitors or an entrance fee. The fact that he kept the house spotless and stark pointed to something more than an aging man holding on to old memories.

José wasn't paranoid, but he knew about the surveillance culture and was sure that every electronic doodad and weird piece of metal was scanned by the authorities on the way in. As long as nothing said *bomb* or *biohazard* he was able to experiment as he saw fit.

Time eternal, passed as it always does, days becoming years. José worked alone on his TimeWall device but was not completely disconnected. He was still part of a loose affiliation of time researchers. They were a bit secretive and never formalized their interactions with an organizational name. Each one strove to be the first to break through the flexible Jello shell of living time.

These researchers seldom went to colloquial meetings, which all too often became fractious, as ideas were tossed around like mortars. Discussions rarely resulted in bloodshed and dueling was limited to brains at close quarters.

Except for the annual Timeless BBQ, most preferred to work in isolation, planning on keeping all the glory for themselves. A few would form small cliques from time to time, although most had trouble sharing hard-earned information, as partnerships frequently dissolved. It was more likely that the isolated researchers would disappear in poverty and unobtrusive quietness, never finding, never giving up on the holy grail of Time itself.

This, of course, did not mean there were no successes in the field. Finding a crack in the ameboid-gel TimeWall wasn't the hard part. Reporting back in a timely manner was.

Every conceivable technique short of splitting atoms was tried by the diverse independent students of time. If they could have gotten their hands on fissionable material, some would have tried that, too.

The next Timeless BBQ rolled around and José had to decide if he was going.

"It's rough without my *madre* around. I wonder if Papa knows about what happened. At least I have *tio* Carlos to help."

Talking to no one wasn't unusual and he knew his Shadows were following his every action.

"It's a good thing I can't hear them. I don't know why most of the conversations beyond Time turned snarky the last time I was there. The discussions always seemed to travel in circles before they got to the point."

His Shadows, mute to José but active among themselves, made their own conclusions about their host's situation.

One of his Shadows, some 10 minutes removed from the front, had thoughts.

>There he goes, complaining about us again.

The neighbor Shadows nodded and mumbled in agreement. The complaining Shadow moved back in the line, his voice and opinions reduced unless carried forward by others.

>Can anyone convince him to go to the BBQ? I'm tired of this cold, damp hole he calls a laboratory.

>>Exactly. I want to see other Shadows and maybe get a touch of brisket.

>>>Good idea. We can pass it down the line.

>Yuck. Partially eaten brisket. That's a memory we could do without.

>>>You're probably right. Does anyone want to trade their place with me? I want to be at the front when the meal starts.

>That's a long time from now. First, José has to get to the BBQ. If only he'd learn to listen to us. We know better.

"I don't know why I'm having such a hard time deciding about the BBQ?" said José. "I need to go, and at least visit the swap table. I can take my *tio* Carlos if he feels up to it.

Too bad he can't cook the brisket anymore. His last girlfriend wasn't much better. I don't think she could even boil water. I guess I'll have to pick up something from the deli."

José spent a few hours picking out gear for the swap table, then drove out to pick up his *tio* before heading out to the Elks club for food and gossip. Carlos carefully opened the heavy door on the Oldsmobile and placed his cane against the dashboard.

"You know, we could have taken my MG," said Carlos. "It still runs good and gets better mileage."

"It's not that far," said José. "I don't mind driving."

José didn't mention that the five-speed manual transmission was not his preferred system. He could probably figure out the clutch, given enough time, but learning how to shift on his *tio*'s favorite car was not something he wanted to explore.

José took out the plate from the deli and did his best to sneak it onto the potluck table. It didn't meet the expected criteria of home-made, culturally accurate food, although in José's case, it probably did.

"Is Hector coming?" asked Carlos. "Or is he lost in Time somewhere?"

"You never know who's going to show up. I don't see anyone from the university. I wonder if that program is still in operation."

"It's not my department, but the scuttlebutt says that Dr. Jamieson's Proton Time Gun exploded during a test run a few years back."

"Was the military there? That would have been fun to see," said José. "I'd like to see Geoff again. At the very least, he would know exactly what happened."

"Look," said Carlos. "There's Hector, hanging out with his military buddies, again."

José waved, and Hector walked over.

"I bet you he brings up his Marine service," said Carlos.

"I won't take that bet, unless you want to do the over/under on how long it takes for him to bring it up? I'll take less than 15 seconds."

"You're on."

"José, Carlos. Glad you could make it. I was just talking to my military friends, swapping stories of my time in the Corps."

Carlos passed a $20 bill to José.

"They sent a bunch of Lieutenants for the meeting. I wasn't impressed with their knowledge," said Hector. "I don't think they know anything about Time, or even want to learn."

"Well, that clinches it," said José "The Proton Time Gun group is officially defunct. I can't say I'm surprised. High-energy protons were never the key to breaking into the TimeWall."

"I'm sure you're right. Sound is the only way to open the TimeWall, if you ask me," said Hector/

"You won't get an argument from me," said José.

"Did you get the data I sent?" said Hector. "It was a huge file and your email might not be able to handle it."

"I got it last week, but haven't had a chance to go over it yet. This week, for sure."

"You should give my protocols a try," said Hector. "I've been able to visualize the TimeWall, but still can't seem to find the key to open it."

"I'm looking forward to seeing what you've come up with," said José. "We can work together after the meeting and find the tweak to get things moving."

"I'd like to try that. Give me a call when you get the chance."

The files were a tantalizing combination of sound, video, and text documenting Hector's time-wall experiments. A recording, spitting out mournful wails, and a list of frequencies and amplitudes were a critical part of the dataset.

Chapter 35 - Time Plus 10

Time continued its journey from its beginning to whatever its end would be, but the TimeExplorers weren't interested in how Time happened or where it was going. They were only concerned with the interface of the Now and before the Now.

To be honest, some of the explorers wanted to break into the future, but even Time didn't know the equation leading in that direction.

It wasn't unusual for this group of inventors and tinkers to go incognito for months at a time, and José hadn't given the lack of communication with Hector a second thought. Only time would tell if he breached the TimeWall or had found some other interest to send him down a different path.

The data José and Hector shared consisted of notes and videos of their trials and failures. The last batch of notes was similar to his current settings.

"These are pretty close to what I've been doing lately. It's not like my experiments have been conclusive. I'll give this a try."

"I need to clear out some workspace. The last thing I need is to mismatch my device with Hector's configuration. It would be safer to build a new machine from scratch. I need a spare anyhow."

The lab space was more like a large closet than a full-fledged laboratory. The detritus from his extended family was carefully packed and labeled against the far wall. Tools hung against one wall and above his workbench, which was surprisingly disorganized for one with such an OCD history.

The workbench was strewn with quantum electronics, vacuum tubes, wires, and metal. Despite the general disarray, the work area was clean. Two large HEPA filters hummed, sucking up all the extraneous fumes, dust, and mites that might damage sensitive equipment.

On the table, his most recent TimeWall machine had its guts strewn out, naked for all to see. Wires and alligator clips connected the disparate parts, allowing the device to sing in its key of banshee.

It didn't take long to replicate his friend's work, and the new machine quickly matched the instructions.

José's gray close-cut hair reflected the purple light from the vacuum tubes clamped in their sockets. He continued his focused research, sampling sounds, building datasets, looking for leaks bleeding through the time barrier.

His working space had room for a vanity wall where photos of his *sobrinos* and *sobrinas* wearing sports gear were carefully placed. His pride was a plaque celebrating his retirement written in gold on a Vantablack background.

NightLite Industries, Inc.
10 years of service for
José Isaac Davidovich

The plaque was the sole memento from his stint at NightLite. A pocket watch would have been a nice gesture, but the skills and knowledge gained over the years were all he needed from the experience. That and a pension.

He was lucky, though. The company was one of the few left that paid a good pension and, as a bonus, medical care. Once he was nominally vested in the system, he was out and ready to go back to doing what he loved, tinkering with Time. His expenses were minimal, the house paid for and he had a basement full of electronics bought and scavenged over the years.

Research is nothing else if not persistent, time-consuming, and boring. With enough sampling, he designed his improved TimeWall-breaking speakers, ready to send the extrapolated noises back to the barrier.

"This is frustrating. Everything seems to work, but the components are a little off. The TimeWall is easy to call up, but I can't make it any bigger than a dime, not the universe-spanning wall I was expecting. It's too bad the vacuum tubes cracked the last time I passed to the Now."

José was not the type to give up, especially after his earlier successes.

"Would super glue work? They look too fragile to make another journey and I wouldn't want to be stuck behind the Now."

No one wants to trust their existence to super glue, in spite of the advertisements. In spite of Hector's notes, it took more than a few weeks to find suitable replacement parts and build the device.

"Hector's version is done as best I can. The new machine works and it might be better than my last one, even if the parts aren't the same."

Now, in the Now, he could open the TimeWall at will and was determined to unleash Time's secrets in what little time he had left on this Earth.

"I wish my *madre* was around to see my latest machine. I know she didn't appreciate the noise, but seeing it in action would help soothe old wounds."

Deep beyond Time's interface his Shadows considered their options.

>Can we help our host? How hard would it be to find the last link to our *madre*?

>>Hard. She's not in the cemetery; her ashes are on a shelf in our host's basement.

>That sounds a little cold. I didn't know he resented his mother.

A distant Shadow moved forward.

>>I think he did it to be close to his *madre*. It's a sign of respect.

>Still, that doesn't make our job any easier. Showing our host his mother's transition to ashes could never be good for him or us.

>>We should let him have his own way. There is nothing we can do from here.

>I know. If he comes back we can ask what he wants.

José was not privy to the Shadow conversations, but thoughts of his family intruded on his plans to go back behind Time.

"I better get some supplies for the trip. I don't think I'll need a sleeping bag. I'm not planning on staying that long."

José went upstairs and started rooting through the cabinets. A sleeve of Fig Newtons, cans of tuna and bread were the only staples.

"I guess I'll make a few sandwiches before I leave. After all, it's only a quick trip to test out the equipment. If everything goes as I expect, I'll contact Hector and we can plan a more extensive outing later. I really need a way to record the trip, but the TimeWall interface always seems to delete the information. At least I have the house and my *madre's* car. I have her to thank for that."

That morning, José loaded up his *madre's* old car with his bike and supplies, then drove north on the narrow road running up the spine of the rolling hills above town. The knoll was high on the ridge line, far from civilization and was José's quiet place. Out there he could run his TimeWall noise-breaker without any questions.

"I wonder if there is anything left of the university's Time Lab. I'm sure the military wanted nothing more to do with it once the Proton Gun exploded."

Chapter 36 -
Time Again

His mother's ancient Oldsmobile was showing its age, no different from José, except his gray hair was holding up better than the car's peeling paint. His youthful interest in electronics paid him back, giving him the skills to keep that ancient hunk of metal in drivable shape.

His bike was better maintained; it was stored in his mother's basement, wrapped in a tarp to keep the dust and any inquisitive mice away. He spent the last week updating his old ride with new tires and took care to polish it to a shiny finish, the candy-apple red tubes glistening in the morning light.

"I'm sure glad I can keep this old car going. It's struggling to get up the hills, I can only imagine how I'd do on my bike."

The car huffed up the winding road to his favorite turnout. A rusting chain blocked off the access road to the university's abandoned TimeLab annex.

"Good," said José. "There are no cars here. The last thing I want to do is disturb anyone left over from a night at the town's impromptu lover's lane."

It was still damp from the morning dew on Now's end of the moving TimeWall. He unpacked his gear and checked power levels.

"I don't know how long I'll stay behind Time, so I better be prepared."

José was never a gourmet and his lack of cooking skills was obvious. He was able to make a mean tuna-fish sandwich with habanero chiles on dill rye just like his *madre* used to prepare. He stuffed a couple of sandwiches, cookies, and some tools in the bike's panniers in case he stayed longer than expected. Pushing a 15kg fat-tire bicycle up an overgrown dirt road with an equally heavy backpack is not an easy task, especially for the elderly. José was an old-school scientist and did things his way, even if it meant exertion that could kill a younger person.

His TimeWall-breaking sound-generating backpack was tuned to local time. The home-built computer interface he added homed in on distinct frequencies and patterns and quickly opened a small human-sized fracture in Time's unending barrier.

No matter how many times he stepped behind the shimmering TimeWall, it was disconcerting seeing the dark-gray string of one-dimensional connected replicants.

"Oh well," said José, "It must be worse for my Shadows to see a 3D copy of their last me."

He got used to the front Shadows swapping faces to show emotion, every piece thin and unique. Each visage held a single expression, but the same mouth which always let him know when his Shadows didn't approve of what he was doing. He knew that he didn't need to speak his thoughts out loud, there was no one around who could hear, but his voice filled the gray, empty space around him and made him feel safer.

At least the interaction with the leading Shadow was consistent, it always appeared angry and embittered at the intrusion.

"Wait," said José. "Isn't the last one a duplicate of my last expression? Do I look like that now?"

The front-facing Shadow was worse than a mirror. It wasn't a reflection on a shiny surface but an exact caricature of his last moment, true to himself.

The front facing Shadow nodded in agreement and stood with the same bike and backpack José had when he stepped behind Time. José smiled, the Shadow's one-dimensional bike didn't sparkle like his tricked-out wheels. *A win for the host*, he thought.

At least he brought his bike this time. Exploration is so much better on a Schwinn. The fat tires and simple five-speed dérailleur let him travel with ease.

"Where do you want to go?" asked José.

The front Shadow answered for the line:

>Does it really matter? We're stuck to you like glue.

151

"Quantum time elastic," said José. He was always precise when talking about concepts and felt it was his duty to correct any misstated fact, even from himself. This trait never failed to impress his friends and family throughout his life, if being shunned by others was a goal.

"Com'on, let's explore. I want to see what TimeWorld is all about."

It was early on both sides of the TimeWall and the bike trail wrapped gently around the grassy mound above the town. On this side of the wall, there were no birds singing, just the gentle buzz of noise slices to indicate that a sound had happened only a moment before. He was at the top of the knoll overlooking the village and had no place to go but down. With his bike, he was able to take shortcuts and the cemetery was in his path, located on a small bluff some distance from the town's center.

"Let's check out the TimeLab first. There might be some interesting equipment I can salvage. If I find anything, I'll come back later if it looks worthwhile."

>You're a little late to the party, buddy. The locals have already looted the place.

The garage door was blown off its hinges and Time's fog filled the rusted-out Quonset hut.

"This looks like it could fall down at any moment. I'll check around, but it doesn't look that safe. When was this abandoned?"

>Take a look. Do you see the purple haze in the distant past?

José peered down past's path. Replicas of the Quonset hut blocked his view, but he could just make out the light of a running Proton Time Gun. A huge ball of purple fog caught his attention.

"Is that where the lab exploded?"

>We don't know, we weren't here. Remember, we are always where you are.

152

"I'd like to forget about that. It can be a little creepy having Shadows follow me around."

>It's even worse for us. We know what you do.

"Let's not go down that path. This place is strange enough without knowing what you Shadows do all day."

>And night too.

"Right. Too much information."

The cleared-out Proton Time Lab was the first obstacle he came across. Old barbed wire fences and abandoned buildings were easy to traverse as only a host could do. The QTmBits were no barrier for the three-dimensional host. His Shadows had to negotiate the mess as best they could.

He stopped on the flat apron in front of the crumbling Quonset hut.

"What a waste," said José. "If they had listened to me, they would have found the key to the Wall. Oh well, it would probably be too crowded with the whole world able to go behind Time."

Chapter 37 -
Time to Ride

José sped down the path and approached the mall. The ride down was interesting, passing through lines of small rocks and trees that had no substance for him.

As usual, his Shadows had different experiences and suffered to keep up with him.

In the distant past, a team of Shadows broke away from the pack and rode parallel to his path, young replicas on the same bike. The unbiked Shadows followed, stretched thin, trying to keep up with only the QTmBit strings keeping them connected.

The dank fog was starting to lift and José peered off into the distance. The town was still a few kilometers away as he came up to the mall's parking lot. Strange squawking caught his attention and he asked his front Shadow about it.

"Are those birds? How come they don't have any connections to the wall? "

>You don't want to meet up with them.

"You forget, I'm a scientist. My job is to learn all I can about the TimeWall. They look like vultures, floating in the fog. Next time I'll bring binoculars."

>Bring some high-powered ones. We need to keep away from them, they're dangerous.

"To you or me?"

>All we've heard is that they eat memories and that's us, if you recall.

"I've been meaning to ask. How do you communicate with other Shadows? It seems you have information that I've never thought of. Aren't you supposed to be replicates of me?

>It's quite simple, if you think about it. Whenever we pass other Shadows we can pick up a little information and vice versa. We all share the information, whatever the source.

"Let me see. You leak information to any other Shadow? Does that mean they are getting smarter and you're getting dumber?"

>That's a little rude. So, you think we're dumb?

José thought, *I better be careful. I don't want my Shadows to rebel. I still need their help to negotiate this strange world.*

"No. Nothing like that. You're as least as smart as I am. I hope you're making the other Shadows smarter. Without losing anything."

A slightly mocking face flipped to the front of the line.

>You bet we're the smart ones.

"Well, I'm not going to worry about the birds. They won't hurt me? Right? I don't see a problem."

More flips and contempt seemed to take the lead.

>Why did we figure out you would say that? Do you want to lose your memories?

"I wouldn't mind forgetting a few bad ones. Can I choose which one of you to go?"

A distant Shadow zipped to the front ready to take charge.

>>Some of us are taking bets on what memories you would choose to lose. Do you want to join the pool?

"No. I'm here for science, not gambling. So far, none of my old memories have proven to be all that useful."

>You say that now. What if you forget how to ride a bike?

"I'm sure I can re-learn that, I'm not a fish, you know."

>Or walk or breathe. We know you need those traits.

"You may have a point. Maybe I'll leave that exploration of those birds for later. Are there any other dangers I need to watch out for?"

A haughty copy replied.

>We're sure you'll find out soon enough.

Some of the more distant Shadows started waving their arms, signaling their desire to add their opinion.

"I see some of the other Shadows have something they want to add to the conversation.

>You don't want to listen to them. They can't tell nightmares from reality.

"You call this reality?" said José.

>Well, it's ours and sorta yours, too.

"Relatively speaking, of course," said José.

155

>Relatively.

"I guess it's okay to ignore them for now. We should be at the mall soon. I'd like to take a look at some of the stores on this side of the Now. Especially the video and electronic stores. I can check out what they have been hiding from me in their back rooms. They never seem to understand what I'm asking for, but I can grab the stock numbers and get the exact part I need."

>That's it? You want to be a stock clerk in the Now? This seems like a lot of effort just to find some old equipment.

I think my Shadows misspoke, thought José. *They really do seem to be getting dumber.*

As José was discussing the validity of IQ points, a few of the distant Shadows moved to the front.

The front Shadows started twitching, fog rising around its head. A new face became the front-facing Shadow.

>Hello, José. Do you remember us? We're from your dreams.

"Nightmares? I thought you were repressed by the other Shadows."

>Funny how we keep on finding a way to the front. In any case, we're here to warn you about the monsters we've seen.

"How do I know you're not just dreaming and have no connection with reality?"

>You don't. You'll just have to trust us. We're here to help you. The Shadows that the other hosts call cryptids live here. They feed off memories and can break through to the Now in the right conditions.

"Like late at night, in dreams?"

>Yes. Except they can be real. Don't you remember the monsters under the bed you were worried about when you were younger?

"No."

>So, you're blocking out those memories? That's okay. Everyone does it.

"Don't tell me, you're the psychologist behind the Now?"

>I guess you could say that. We have nothing much else to do. Analyzing memories keeps us busy.

"And a little psychotic, I bet."

>It is a little boring here. Waiting for you to do something interesting.

"Good to know. I'll try to be more flamboyant. I don't want bored Shadows.

>You would do that for us? It would be wonderful. Can you learn to dance?

>>With a girl?

"I'll keep that in mind. Right now I have more exploring to do. If you don't have any specific warnings, you can come along at your pleasure. I'm going to visit my mall stores behind the Now."

>We'll come along. Do you want suggestions on where the good stuff is kept?

"Just don't get in my way."

Chapter 38 -
Time for Colonists

José continued to the central business district. It was no longer a dirt path rolling down the hills, but a gray shadow-sidewalk running around the back of the shopping mall.

"This is much better," said José. "My old bike is sturdy, but it does much better on a paved surface. The mall seems quiet for a change. Good thing I don't want to see my shadows commingled with a bunch of shopping mall strangers."

His Shadows on their bike copies were riding comfortably on the extended concrete apron. José was moving fast enough to feel the dense fog on his face.

"I've almost gotten used to the moldy, stinky fog, but now it's even worse. I thought the sewage plant was on the other side of town, down by the river. Did it get moved when I wasn't looking or is this unique to TimeWorld?"

He looked over to his trailing Shadows, but none appeared to notice the odor.

"What fun, I'm the only one who can smell these noxious fumes."

Wait, thought José. *How come the sewage plant has to have a stinky shadow? I would think it wouldn't be necessary here or at least it shouldn't smell. I guess TimePhysics requires odors? That is something else to explore or better yet, leave it to future TimeExplorers who don't mind stinky air.*

He kept cycling down the path, keeping near the back edge of the mall's loading docks, trying to outrun shadow smells. His Shadows, on the other hand, just needed to keep up, pulled along by their attached QTmBits.

His bike was running silent on the shadow sidewalk and he was able to hear everything in the immediate environment. Still no birds, just the rough beat of songs, a time slice apart. The tinnitus of nature helped hide his presence.

He rounded a corner behind a loading dock and pulled up short. A few meters away were a couple of small tents set up behind a small fire facing the mall. Some of the tents appeared to be nothing more than gray tarps held up by small sticks. A tripod held a dark pot, steam coming around the lid.

"I never saw this encampment on the Now side of Time before. I guess I missed it by driving instead of biking. That's okay, I'm getting too old to huff it up a hill for fun. I'd rather drive than see every small detail on the side roads."

The camp was huddled on the apron leading up to a loading dock, with some of the shelters sitting on the shadow dirt at the back of the mall.

"Maybe the mall can't afford security anymore. It's been looking a bit run-down lately. I'm surprised that the owners approved the camp."

The campers were gathered around a cooking pot and no one noticed José and his red bike. One of the campers tossed a gray block into the pot.

"If that's food, then I know why it smells so bad here. Glad I've got my bike so I can move on quickly."

There was no connection to a host on the other side of Time and José knew that only the dead and TimeExplorers like himself had no shadow links leading back to the moving TimeWall.

"Well, they do look human at least, but what are they doing here? There's a whole string of shadows hanging off the back end, but I don't see anything linked to the TimeWall. I hope they're not cannibals or if they are, not hungry."

One of the campers stood up and waved in José's general direction. He waved back and the whole group turned to face him.

"They don't look like the newly dead," said José. "And they look three-dimensional. Are they from my side of the TimeWall? I better be careful."

José stepped off the bike and approached one of the occupants. "Hello, my name is José Isaac Davidovich, Time Explorer. To whom do I have the pleasure of addressing?

The campers were dressed in loose clothing, almost like ponchos, with muted shadow-like colors.

José thought, *Seems like a homeless style. I wonder how they got here. I don't see any electronic gear.*

159

One of the better-dressed campers said, "Welcome to our little camp. My nombre is Petra Mangenue. Did you just fall through the TimeWall?"

A small camper, childlike, looked up from behind an adult and asked, "Did you bring any food?"

José thought, *If I give them food, they may accept me into the group. That has to be better than being tossed in the pot as their next meal.*

He reached into the bike's panniers and took out a small lunch bag.

"I have a tuna sandwich and some cookies. Here, these are Fig Newtons. Would you like one?"

The child camper grabbed the cookie and ran away with her prize. Her Shadows followed, but there was still no connection upstream to the TimeWall.

"I didn't expect to see any other hosts here," said José. "Did you use a TimeWall breaking machine like mine?"

"What's that?" said Petra. "No one here used a mechanical device, each one of us fell through the wall and can't get back."

"That's rough," said José. "Was it all at the same time? Maybe there's a connection that will help explain the TimeWall."

"Each of us came at different times. It's random as far as we can tell, years or months apart, and there is never a pattern we've noticed."

"Have you tried to return?" asked José

"Of course," said Petra. "But it's been so long most of us have given up trying. We're committed to living here. It isn't that bad, peaceful even."

"I would have to try to go back to the Now," said José. "It seems a little boring here."

"Well, we like it. We've seen what happens in the Now and don't care to mingle with the people we see at the mall."

One of the campers spoke up. "I miss TV. There was a video store on this dock and we could watch shows through the windows."

Petra admonished the TV addict, "You know we can't control the Now. Complaining doesn't improve our situation."

160

"If you don't mind me asking, how do you get food?"

The camper by the pot said, "It's not hard. If we stay here at the mall we can grab any food as soon as the TimeWall passes. If you toss it into hot water, it's fine to eat."

"So that's why you're parked next to the mall," said José.

"Exactly. New food for the taking. Water is from the spring they covered up when they built the mall. We dug a trench on this side of Time and have an ample supply."

José had a memory flash of his *tio* talking about water ghosts, *La Llorona* and other water spirits.

Is that my Shadows forcing a memory out? That's a bit rude if you ask me.

"That sounds about perfect," said José. "Although a little dull for my tastes."

"We move camp every other day or so. Some days behind Time are so nice, we like to hang out and do nothing.

"Sounds like a permanent vacation," said José. *Interesting. They seem to do nothing all day, and they've developed it into an art form.*

José asked, "Doesn't it take a while to break up camp and move forward? What happens if you wait too long?"

"It isn't much of a walk," said Petra. "Distances are compressed the closer you are to the TimeWall and things move slower on this side. We only have to move every couple of days. When we leave for the winter, we find a road and travel laterally next to the TimeWall. It doesn't take long at all."

"At the speed of Time?" asked José

"I suppose so, now that you mention it," said Petra.

José couldn't get over the smells of the cooking shadow food, akin to the smells of old socks and older meat. He couldn't refrain from asking an obvious question.

"What happens to the garbage and waste?"

"It stays, we go."

"That explains the odors around here," said José.

"It can get a bit strong, especially in the summer," said Petra.

"Let me see if I have this correct," said José. "You make camp and then after the TimeWall moves on, you have to keep walking, over and over?"

"Yes. We don't mind and since we're hosts, the *Chupacabra* won't bother us.

"The what? Don't tell me you're afraid of myths?"

The campers looked at each other before Petra spoke. "For you it's a myth. I'm sure it won't bother you… much."

Chapter 39 - Time for Fire

Conversation stalled. It seemed to José that the campers had some superstitions and he might have stepped on one. Another camper spoke up to break the impasse.

"Did you know you could bounce into the Time Wall? If you do it right, Time wiggles. Little kids can see it and some of them get scared enough to drop their food. I love summer. And ice cream."

A younger camper said, "Some of the hosts like to sit on the staff picnic table and read books or scroll the Internet. We like to look over their Shadow's shoulder."

"I hate the fast readers," said one of the other campers.

"It must be fun keeping up with society, but not being part of it," said José. "Does this explain the lost sock conundrum?"

"I guess," said Petra. "Now that you mention it, we always have socks."

"Do you get many visitors here?" asked José

Petra said, "I've been here the longest, over a thousand cycles, and I know we haven't had anyone new for many cycles."

This generated more questions than answers.

"I'm not sure of your counting system. Is a cycle one dark-to-light sequence, like a day on the other side of Time?"

The old woman giggled, "No, no. A cycle is a turn around the sun, just like on your side. Do you see where the shadow day/night cycles compress to a point on the horizon?"

José looked to the past and saw the never-ending rings of dark and light coming to a dull point in the fog.

"Time is compressed the farther away it is from the Now. That distance is around one hundred of Now's years.

"Wow. Do you mean your history goes back over a thousand years? Do you have records?"

"We're not the best at jotting things down. Every turn of the Earth is the same for us. I've been here the whole time," said Petra.

"A thousand years?"

"Yes, and a little more. The others have been here less."

"How does that happen?" asked José. "Aren't you a host with a finite life span? Did you have to die on the Now side of Time to get here?"

"I don't think so," said Petra. "I didn't see my body spread out on a slab, so there's that. The best we've been able to figure out is that the TimeWall burped and we're here."

"You're welcome to stay here," said one of the campers. "We have story time every seven days. We'd love to have some new stories."

"Or a TV," said another camper.

"Let me get this straight," said Petra. "You didn't come here by accident? How can that happen? Are you a witch or do you have a familiar who opened Time for you?"

José took a step back.

"Not quite, I constructed a device that lets me open the TimeWall. Anyhow, I don't think magic is real, I use science."

"Science? I've heard about that. I think it's new," said Petra. "I'm sure the rest of the campers would like to hear your story. Can you show us some science? Do you have any with you?

"My Time rig is all built on science, but I'd rather not have anyone tinker with it," said José. "In any case, I must continue exploring this realm. Time waits for no one, I've heard."

"If you can't stay," said Petra. "Will you join us for tea and snacks before you leave?"

José's Shadows flipped, ending on a face mouthing "NO!"

"If you insist," said José.

The whole camp assembled for morning tea. There were only five people and a small dog.

Clear, cold shadow spring water filled the tea pot and gray bricks were added to the fire to keep the water boiling.

"Where do you get the fire bricks?" asked José. "I don't see any trees around here."

"We don't need trees. When the mall is busy we simply grab a few passing shadows and roll them up as logs. It takes a few days for them to dry out, but they burn great."

José said, "That's real strange. Doesn't it hurt the host?"

"Nah. They seem fine. You can barely hear them scream when we burn them. What's a few lost memories? A couple of stiff drinks will do the same."

"I suppose," said José, thinking. *This group seems completely off the rails. Glad I don't like coming to the mall.*

Shadow tea was a little off. It sort of had a flavor, but was a bit gritty. José nodded to his host and smiled, trying not to make it into a grimace.

"The tea takes a little getting used to," said Petra. "You'll start to enjoy it the longer you stay here."

José smiled, hoping that everyone couldn't hear his guts gurgling as the shadow liquid merged with his real stomach lining.

José looked around for a polite way to dump his tea. There were no potted plants nearby so he gently set down the cup. *It would probably kill a plant anyhow*, he thought. *I can wait until no one is looking and dump it on the ground.*

It was getting close to sunset in Now Time and the camp was getting dark.

"Don't you have to move camp to keep up with the TimeWall?" asked José.

"We're in no rush. Since space gets constricted the closer you get to the TimeWall, we can cover a couple of Now-days' worth of walking in a few hours. That's why we keep the gear light and easy to pack.

"That's good to know. Maybe I can explore deeper into TimeWorld. At least I'll be able to get back fairly quickly."

Petra said, "Be careful out there. There are hazards not found in the Now that you'll have to deal with and they can cause you and your shadows a lot of grief."

"Like what?" asked José. "My *tio* mentioned *La Llorona* and *Chupacabra,* but those are just fairy tales."

"*La Llorona* doesn't exist, as far as we know. There are some water spirits who hang out at the spring, but as long as you go down there during the day, they'll leave you alone."

The little girl chimed in. "They're my friends. We play tag all the time."

165

"Water spirits?" asked José. "That sounds a lot like *La Llorona*. Where did they come from? I can't believe they were from the other side of Time and ended up here."

"My water friends told me they are leftover memories," said the little girl.

"That's right," said Petra. "The spring used to be a roaring river many cycles ago. People have died in the water and some of the memories are persistent. After ages, they are pale, ghost images of their hosts."

"I should go talk to them," said José. "I'd like to write about that phenomenon."

"We wouldn't advise it," said Petra. "You can ask your shadows, those ghostly images have a bad reputation here."

"But they're my friends. They've never hurt me," said the little girl. "They like to play tag."

Petra said, "I guess they're comfortable with the young hosts. I think it would be a risk for you."

"It sounds like it isn't healthy to be disconnected from your memories," said José.

José turned to his leading Shadow. "Is that true?"

>Yes. Every Shadow knows that. Leaving the group and breaking the QTmBit connections can lead to mental issues for the host and their Shadows.

As if everything isn't mental around here already, thought José

"Don't worry," said Petra. "The water spirits only attack after daylight. They can pass to the Now in the dark and frighten hosts. Normally, they stay in the spring, but if they get uncomfortable, they'll attack any living thing."

"Jealous of the living, I bet," said José. "It seems that they might be trying to join a host's Shadow stream. I wouldn't want them hanging around my memories, that's for sure."

Petra said, "Spending cycles roaming around, looking for missing Shadows does seem to send them over the edge."

"They can be dangerous, but they're easy to avoid, just don't cross water at night," said one of the campers.

"So, they're in every water source?" asked José.

"We don't know, we keep to the same paths cycle after cycle and don't go looking for trouble. If you find out, you can let us know."

"Well, that is quite informative," said José. "Are there any other cryptids I need to worry about?"

"Hardly anything, it's quite safe back here."

Another camper chimed in, "Ancient birds can be a problem."

"Pterodactyls?"

"Those are rare, but the larger eagles like Haasts, can be a problem," said Petra. "Fortunately, we're nowhere near New Zealand and I don't think many have made the journey over here."

"Oh. I must find those," said José. "Think of the paper I can publish in the Now. The paleontologists would die to get a look."

"They just might," said Petra.

Chapter 40 -
Time for Merchants

José looked up and saw a group of Shadows stumbling toward the camp.

"Are those more campers?" asked José. "I don't see a host or a connection to the TimeWall."

The group walked slowly toward the camp, weird banshee singing announced their presence.

"Ignore them," said Peter." They're lost memories wandering around looking for a host."

"Like zombies?" said José. "I'll ask my Shadows. They should know more about these beasts."

"Hey, me. What's going on?"

>You better step back. We don't know what they are. Don't let them touch us. You could lose memories, and that means us.

"I'm real disappointed with you, Shadows," said José. "You've been here all my life and you still don't know what's going on."

>Don't blame us. We're just a reflection of you.

"That's what I keep on hearing. Don't you have any initiative? You're supposed to be scientists, like me."

>It's not like we can drive the equation. We're the past, you're the present and the future. We have enough trouble dealing with what you do every day.

"Let's not go into that right now," said José. "We can discuss your issues about my lifestyle later, if you don't mind."

"Don't worry," said Petra." They're traders, not zombies. They traffic in fine, selected memories. The worst they can do is add to your past. They will become part of your memory pool. Sometimes they are fun to have around."

José's Shadows had a different opinion.

>Jump on your bike, those shuffling zombies can't keep up.

The lead Shadow of the wanderers got closer to José, dragging its string of memory shadows.

A smiling face spoke from the unfettered memories.

>>Don't listen to your Shadows. We're not Zombies. We can't hurt you or your Shadows. We're simply sellers of exquisite memories. And for your pleasure we have some very famous Shadows.

"Why should I trust you? I don't even know you. At least my Shadows are looking after my interests."

>>We have Max Planck and other notables.

"That's all well and good, but isn't there a cost for those memories," said José. "What's the currency here? Do you take credit cards?"

The zombie merchant replied.

>>Not even cash works here. All we have are Shadows. We buy and sell them. I'm sure you have some wonderful memories you don't need to keep.

"So, I pay with my memories. No thanks."

>>You'll hardly miss a few old memories. Since you're a host, I can give you an excellent exchange for fresh Shadows. Say, five of your shadows for one of our curated memories."

José's Shadows quickly flipped faces. Worry was in the front.

>Don't do it. We want to stay here, with you, not be sold like cattle.

"I think not," said José. "My Shadows are precious to me."

His front-facing Shadows flipped expressions again, tones brightly filling the fog and a broad smile led the pack.

>>Think of the opportunity you'd be passing up. You could have memories of a great thinker. It can only help you in your career and might make you smarter."

"I can send them away, if you want," said Petra. "But first, we need to ask for your help."

"Sounds like a *quid pro quo* request," said José. "What happens if I don't agree to your terms? Will you have the zombies attack me?

"Nothing like that," said Petra. "We would just like you to visit when you're back in the Now. Maybe bring some real food."

"And cookies," said the little camper.

"That doesn't sound like too much of an ask. I can try to do it when I'm in the neighborhood. Now how are you going to make the zombies leave?" José asked. "Don't tell me you're a wizard?"

"No. Nothing like that," said Petra. "We're friends. A little food, some tea, and they'll be on their way."

"How do I know they won't try to steal some of my Shadows when our paths cross?"

The merchant leader bristled at the suggestion.

>>That's insulting. We're honest traders. We would never steal.

"You know, you should consider their offer," said Petra. "They have all sorts of memories, sometimes from actual famous people. You can ask them what's in their inventory. Do you have anyone's memory you'd like to have?"

"I think the price would be too high," said José. What do they want in exchange? Nothing seems to be free in TimeWorld."

"Like the Now world is?" said Petra.

"I guess so," said José. Even the swap table at the Timeless BBQ wasn't free. Everyone was expected to bring something of value in trade."

"It's a tiny cost, only a few of your memories," said Petra. "Something you don't want or care about. The value depends upon how much the trade is worth to you."

José's Shadows let them know their feelings on this exchange.

>DO NOT DO THIS!

"I don't know. There are a few memories I'd like to leave behind."

His Shadows recoiled, and stepped back as far as their QTmBit connections would allow.

"Maybe not," said José. "My Shadows don't seem to approve and I have to live with them."

As they were talking, the Shadow entrepreneur moved closer to José's line of Shadows.

"Keep away from them!" yelled José. "My Shadows are bigger and stronger than you. I can have them attack if you don't back off."

170

The offending merchant stopped as a few of José's team gathered round. A small static spark from the combined shadows lashed out. One of the offending Shadows screamed and rapidly turned to gray dust.

>>Okay. Okay. We're going. No need to get rough.

"Sorry," said José. "I didn't authorize that attack. I don't know what got into my Shadows."

>>It's fine," said the lead Shadow. "We didn't care much for that memory anyhow."

The traveling memories coiled like a tightened spring and quickly moved toward the TimeWall, sliding around the camp and José.

"Petra, I apologize for the actions of my Shadows," said José.

"Don't think anything of it. Those merchant memories can be quite annoying. We're all glad you chased them away."

Another camper added, "They often overstay their welcome and when they start singing their banshee songs, it's hard to get them to stop."

"Interesting," said José. "I've been hearing the banshee singing for years. Is that where it's coming from?"

Petra thought about it for a short time. "As far as we know. They are experts on being annoying on either side of Now."

"Good to know. Maybe I'll study them and write a paper on it. I'm sure that would be fun."

Chapter 41 -
Time to Decamp

The memory market moved away, snake-like, singing the songs of the banshees.

Petra said, "We're all friends here at our camp. Everyone here gets along, hosts and shadows."

José's Shadows whispered,

>Don't listen to her. We've talked to some of their Shadows. Something's not right here.

Petra overheard and said, "You can't trust Shadows, even your own. They have their own agenda and can cause trouble if you're not in control."

"You might have a point," said José. "Some of my memories have been quite off-putting. I've never understood where they came from. It's as if my dreams are being manufactured by an outside source."

Petra said, "Who are you going to believe, your fellow host or some random Shadow?"

José's Shadows puffed up, ready for a snappy comeback when José said, "They're not random, they're my Shadows. I think I can trust them."

The other campers moved closer to José and Petra.

"I have a proposal," said Petra. "We need you to do something for us in the Now and we'll return the favor."

"What do you have to trade?" asked José. "Not tea, I hope."

"Memories," said Petra. "We buy them from the roaming merchants and save them so they won't degrade. We have some real exotic ones. We can part with ten."

"How do you pay for them?" asked José. "Are they stolen from travelers or from your own supply?"

"We didn't steal them," said Petra. "We swap our old memories, or if we're lucky, pizza from the staff mall parties, and only a piece or two. There are an unlimited number of Shadows wandering around. We have our pick of the highest quality ones. Do you really think you're the only buyer of Shadows? You're not the first host to wander by."

"Who?" said José "I need to know."

"We have our integrity," said Petra. "We don't share that type of information."

"Okay, how about when? This cycle?"

The smaller camper spoke up. "I remember. It was tens and tens of cycles ago. They had nice horses. I got to pet one."

"Oh. Now I remember," said another camper. "It was before this valley was invaded by the settlers."

"I wish they would come back again, I'd like to visit with the horses," said the little camper. "They said I could ride one when I was bigger."

José did some quick calculations and thought, *before the 1800s from the sound of it.*

"The offer's still on the table," said Petra. "Do you want to trade some of your Shadows for names and times? I'll give you the pick of our inventory."

"With all due respect, I was looking for information on recent hosts, like other TimeExplorers."

"You'll never know who and when unless you pay," said Petra.

"I don't think so. My Shadows aren't comfortable with that type of exchange and I think I have to go."

"How about we trade twelve from our stock and I'll throw in the information you want in exchange for two of your Shadows?"

"There is no number you can give me," said José. "Let's go Shadows. We have more of this world to explore. Good day to you Petra, campers."

Before José could mount his bicycle and speed away Petra called out.

"Wait! Come back and open the wall, we'll break into the deli and stock up."

"No."

"Look," said Petra, "All we're asking is that you walk in the deli, open the TimeWall and we'll take care of the rest. No one would even have to know."

"Except everyone within earshot. I guess you don't know my Time device uses sounds, and it's loud."

"What's the problem? The Hosts on the other side will just think it's sirens. Once the TimeWall opens, they'll run away."

173

"And where does that leave me?"

"You can come with us. We have a nice life beyond Time. No worries, no jobs, an easy life."

"And no plumbing, apparently," said José.

"Not a problem," said Petra. "As I said, waste travels back in time. We don't have to worry about it."

"Now I know where all the bad smells come from," said José. "That's why I don't eat at the mall stores."

"We're used to it. It's no worse than all the other rotting smells beyond Time."

"So, your plan is to migrate along with the TimeWall, forever? Don't your Shadows mind?

"Nah," said Petra. "They're broken in and they sort of like it now. No surprises, just follow the TimeWall. You know, go with the flow."

José's leading Shadow shook his head.

His Shadow whispered,

>We've checked in on the camper's Shadows, they're about to revolt. You better clear out.

"Thank you for the fine tea," said José. "But I have a world to explore and not much time."

Petra chuckled, "We disagree."

A younger camper said, "Can you do us a favor when you get back to Now?"

"I suppose so, as long as it is legal and doesn't hurt my Shadows."

"Do you see that window in the loading dock? Can you place a TV there?"

"I guess I can do that. What channel do you want?"

"Surprise us. You can come back and change the channel every few weeks. It would cost you nothing but a little of your time."

"I'll see what I can do," said José. "But now I must be going."

Buzzing sounds increased as they talked, as lines of Shadows entered from the right, drawing attention to the Now where a group of people were setting up the staff picnic table.

"Look," said one of the campers. "The workers are on a break, it looks like they have pizza."

"We must be going," said Petra. "We're all hungry and can't pass up an easy meal."

"What! Don't tell me you're attacking these Hosts for use as firewood?" said José. "After they brought you pizza."

"Nothing like that," said Petra. "Shadow food, right after it passes the TimeWall is delicious. Come join us."

José said, "That's a relief. I would hate having a chunk of my Shadows eaten, no matter how good it might taste."

"We're not savages, you know. Most of us have developed quite a sophisticated palate over the cycles. You'd be surprised at the number of fancy meals we've been able to partake in."

"And pizza, too," said one of the younger campers.

Back in the Now, a group of workers gathered around the picnic table laid with a checkered tablecloth and covered with boxes of hot pizza.

"Look at that crowd, there must be ten or more," said José. "What happens when the Shadows cross? Is there a risk of merging?"

Petra said, "Not really, we just pass, like ships in the night. The QTmBits know what to do and who to communicate with."

"You're telling me that crossing Shadows spill their guts to anyone who asks?"

"No, not like that," said Petra. "Well, maybe a little, but it's fine. Really it is. Just fine."

José's lead Shadow shook his head in disbelief.

>Don't worry, we wouldn't be so rude as to do that. Fortunately, you're such a loner, we haven't had to deal with that problem very often.

"You're welcome," said José.

The faces flipped and an explainer was front and center.

>It isn't hard. We do it all the time. A little "excuse me's," a few elbows and we manage to pass intact.

"You never meet bad actors? What if they try to steal memories, or worse, Shadows?"

>It's all a reflection of what's in the Now. The usual group of narcissists, lovers, haters, and simply bad attitudes you see everywhere.

"Is that supposed to reassure me? No wonder I've always kept away from crowds."

175

>Don't shoot the messengers, we're here no matter what and have little influence in this world. Pretty much the same as you in the Now.

"Not quite, I can learn and do new things," said José. "You're lucky to be part of me."

His Shadows didn't have a response. They knew their Host could pull the plug on them, probably in the name of 'science.'

"One more reason to keep on moving. TimeWorld is interesting but it sure doesn't sound like heaven," said José.

He secured his TimeWall device, tightened the panniers and jumped on his bike. "The campers look occupied. A few spins of the wheel and they won't be able to catch me."

José passed by the loading dock apron and joined the main trail down toward town.

"I'd better be on the lookout for more campers. I don't want to be caught up in their world or worse."

Chapter 42 -
Time Springs

"It's not dark yet, and I have time to kill. I'd like to learn more about the water sprites. I'm sure if the little girl isn't afraid of them, they won't hurt me."

The spring was slightly uphill from the camp, and José followed the open trench that led down to the campsite.

It wasn't so much a trench as an indentation in the gray soil. Each beat of the TimeWall moved the hole forward, forming a single trench line receding in the distance.

Shadow water flowed in the open trenches, but he could see where the trench near the TimeWall held clear, clean almost-Now water.

"Well, at least they won't die of thirst, as long as the spring holds out."

"I'm sure the water is real, at least for a while. I wonder what H_2O becomes behind the Now? Would it be H_2O_S or $S(H_2O)$ or does it maintain its molecular structure? Is it safe to drink? What I really need is a Mass Spec to test this out. Somehow, I don't think a sample would stay intact if I brought it back to the Now. And I forgot to bring any sampling vials. Oh well, next time."

He could hear the bubbling of the spring and a soft undertone of quiet wailing.

"Those must be the sprites. I don't want to wait around till dark. Maybe if I toss a stone into the spring, they will honor me with their presence."

The Shadows behind him started gesticulating, but José didn't see them or was purposely ignoring his memories. He turned, looking for the perfect pebble and his Shadows said,

>We don't think that is a good idea.

"You're all a bunch of scaredy cats. I'm sure you didn't pick that up from me."

>We beg to differ. Do you want proof?

"No, that's okay. I'll take your word on it. You do know that the living grow and change as they get older. I'm no longer afraid of the things that used to bother me when I was younger."

>You're not that old. It would only take a moment to bring up the right Shadow. Are you sure you don't want to relive those memories? It'll be fun.

"Hey. I'm still the host. Don't I get a say in what memories I get to see?"

>Sure. If you want to be pedantic about it. You can have a say in what you remember.

José tossed his found pebble into a pool near the top of the spring.

>You're not listening to us. Are you? We're not responsible for what happens with the water sprites. They can be mean to strangers.

"That's why I'm the host and you're just faded memories. I'm still in charge. I decide the risks I'm willing to take."

>Be nice. We're all you have.

"Let's see if you can help me for a change. Do the sprites have names? Should I call them *La Llorona*? Is that singular or plural? *La Lloronas* sounds a little strange. Would it be an insult to use a formal name? Or maybe it would be an insult if I don't use that name? What if they are from a different culture? Do they have other names?"

>You should have read up on cryptids before you came. Didn't they teach you how to do research in school?

"Now you're being snotty. Cryptozoology is something hardly anyone studies. I must say, the social norms in this world are almost as bad as in the regular one."

The pool started bubbling and spitting water.

"Hey, me's. Help me out here. Should we run or stick around for science?"

His front Shadow turned backward, molecular fog animated the discussions.

>We took a vote. Run!

"Can you explain why? What do you know that you're not sharing? This is an interesting phenomenon. I'm going to stay and check it out."

>You said it earlier, we're frightened of these sprites. We've never met them, but we have feelings that make up our cultural zeitgeist. Our feelings say run away. What if they feed off of memories?

"So I'll be safe? Good to know."

>They might hurt you, too. Please listen to us. You should take better care of yourself and us. We're not ready to leave this world. Or yours either.

"So far, you Shadows have been a font of bad advice and maligned memories. I think my ideas are better than your past traumas."

Faces flipped, looking for the right responder.

>Suit yourself, we're here no matter what.

The ripples in the puddle died down, with nothing to show for it.

"Where are those sprites? The water has shown nothing exciting. I don't want to stay here all night. I didn't bring enough supplies for a long stay. I guess I should have thought of that before I opened the TimeWall.

>You'll be happy to know we were able to check out ShadowPedia and it says that *La Llorona* brings bad luck to whoever sees it. We should go.

"You have a library? I need to see that! Where is it?"

>You can't get there from here. It's not for hosts.

"I'm sure these are just the lost children. What damage could they do?

>How about we ask someone instead of risking your own Shadows on the unknown.

"This spring looks too little to host a raging monster. I'm sure the sprites here would bring good luck."

>You call yourself a scientist and are dependent on luck? That sounds a bit random.

"What's wrong with luck? It's a feature, not a bug.

>Don't tell us you're willing to risk your poor, innocent Shadows on something as thin as luck? What if *La Llorona* is angry and thinks you're attacking her children?

"I'll take that risk. I thought the Shadows knew about the Einstein Discrepancy Theorem. It isn't luck, it's organized random chance.

>Prove it.

"If I could do that, I wouldn't be hanging out beyond Time. Maybe when I get back to the Now I'll take a crack at it. How hard could it be?"

>We're still uncomfortable near this pond. Nothing good can come from it.

"Not even something to drink? Wouldn't you like a nice glass of cool ShadowWater?"

>Okay, Time Expert. We don't drink or eat. We only exist because you do. Don't forget, we voted and we want to leave.

"What if I veto your vote? I can do that, right?

>Yes, but don't do that.

"Well, you might have a point. I'm bored waiting for old faded memories to appear. They're not even mine."

José saddled up and continued down the hiking trail toward town. As he left, the water stirred and an almost transparent Shadow poked its head out of the pond, watching him and his Shadows leave.

Chapter 43 -
Time Flies

The trail ran adjacent to the town's nature preserve. The land was set aside when the mall was built as a *quid pro quo* exchange for destroying grasslands and part of the watershed. The preserve was bordered with a low fence and kissing gates on the corners to keep out cars, motorcycles, and horses. It did the same for José and his bike.

"This is interesting. There are probably a lot of animals in the preserve. I should check out how they are dealing with this weird Time world. Do they even notice?"

>You can't get your bike through the gate. We should go around.

"Around to where? The fence surrounds the whole preserve.

>You can break through the fence at the back. No one will notice.

"I can do it in the front, too. There is no one but me and my Shadows."

>There are wild animals. We recommend that you don't go.

"Pshaw. I'm not afraid of Shadow animals. I'm sure they won't hurt you either.

>Based on what? We've never been in there before.

"Don't worry, we'll find out soon. If I can't feed the bike through the gate, I'll lift it over."

>You're not as young as you used to be. Are you sure you can lift it over the fence? It must weigh 30kg.

"I know how much it weighs. Just watch me."

It was as simple as lifting the bike over his head, maneuvering through the twisted gate, and not collapsing in a heap or suffering the jab of splinters.

His Shadows simply walked through the Shadow fence as if it didn't exist.

>You made it. We're surprised. We thought it would be harder, given your age and disposition.

"Have some faith in your host. Now let's go explore the preserve, if you're done harassing me."

Dirt and grass are the same on either side of time. Pebbles and rocks became hillocks running back to the past. José did his best to avoid the bigger rocks, but riding through the small Shadow mounds didn't seem to have any effect on him or the rock.

José stopped in front of a one-meter-tall mound blocking his path.

"This must be a huge rock in NowWorld. Am I going to have to carry my bike over my head for every boulder?"

He carefully nosed the bike wheel into the mound until the front wheel touched the rock.

"This is just like the little rocks," said José. "I can ride right through it."

After a few meters of traveling through large rock mounds, José said, "You know, Shadows, I could have simply walked through the gates. Why didn't you tell me it was an option?"

Faces flipped, singing a happy tune.

>Because it was funny.

José sighed, "Check out the string of birds, it looks like they're skywriting."

>You know, we're a string of Shadows, too. How is it different from us?

"You don't fly."

>And whose fault is that? You're the creative scientist. Can't you invent an anti-gravity belt?"

"Sorry. I don't do Flash Gordon, or any other fantasy science. I'd think that opening Time was enough."

>It hasn't helped us any. We want to fly, free as a bird.

"Tell you what. I'll work on it when I get back to the Now. How does that sound?"

>We expected better. But if that's the best you can do…

The Shadow voice trailed off to a sigh.

José thought, *That sounds just like my madre, and I would end up doing whatever she wanted.*

"It is. Now be quiet for a bit so I can check out the preserve."

The Shadows kept still, checking out the scenery, worried about what would happen in this new area.

"Make yourselves useful. Do you know why that bird is not connected to the TimeWall?"

>Which bird? There are so many shadow trails, it's hard to pick one from another.

"The one with the swept-back wings."

His shadows did their usual face flipping looking for an answer. A younger face with binoculars around its neck became the front face.

"Oh, good. I forgot I used to do bird-watching. You, bird-boy. What is that bird?

>Jonathan Seagull?

"Funny, but no. I still know the difference between a seagull and a raptor."

Shadow binoculars raised to shadow eyes tracked the bird.

>That's an osprey. It must be looking for fish.

"How can it live on old Shadow fish?"

The osprey, tired of diving in a shadow pond for shadow fish, noticed José and his tasty Shadows and began an attack run.

>We're under attack!

"I'm sure that little bunch of flying feathers can't hurt us. I still want to explore the preserve."

There was no wind and the osprey had a straight shot to its target.

Claws grabbed a Shadow. Its screams echoed in the timeless fog.

The shock of losing a memory ran up and down José's line of Shadows.

"That hurt. I guess it's time to go."

>You just figured that out? Get on your bike and take us out of this horrible place.

"Is that another osprey? It must be its mate, how interesting."

>Interesting, our asses. Take us out of here.

>Watch out. Here comes another one. It's a feeding frenzy and we're on the menu. Do something, throw a rock.

José looked around for something to use as a weapon.

"There are no solid rocks here, shadow rocks have no substance."

>We don't care, it's your job. That's not how it works. You have to protect your memories, or we're all lost.

"What can I do? I'm not from here."

>Find something before we're all carved up for bird seed.

José started rooting around the panniers looking for anything resembling a solid weapon.

"I'm not going to throw away my bike tools; I may need them later. There's a tuna-fish sandwich. I could use that."

>Anything. Just throw it.

"Wait a minute. Let me take a bite first, I'm hungry."

>Are you stupid? Your memories are about to be eaten. We need help.

"First, one little bite."

José wadded up a piece of the leftover sandwich and tossed it in the general direction of the attacking fowl.

The bird changed its attack and grabbed a fish sandwich on the fly.

>It took the bait. Let's get out of here.

"You know," said José. "They're birds. They can follow us. What if it wants another sandwich?"

>How about we don't sit around and wait to see if it wants seconds?

"Fine, we'll leave the park. There are other places to see. I can come back later."

>Bring a gun next time

"Nah. I don't like guns, I'll just make more sandwiches."

His Shadows did not let the issue go.

>Why did you bring us here? You should have known there were wild Shadow-eating birds flying around.

"And how was I supposed to do that?"

>You've been to the nature preserve, haven't you?

"No. This is the first time that I can recall. I'm sure there is a memory of it somewhere. Can you find it?"

>No. We're not going to stop here and check. Now get out of here, ride like the wind.

Chapter 44 -
Time's Graveyard

José drops down from the nature preserve and continues on the bike path, winding down toward the center of town. Before he can check out downtown, he has to pass through the cemetery.

There's a newly dug grave a few time-slots downstream. José swings wide behind the mourners hovering around the final resting site of a newly interred person. Shadows intermingle as the mourners shuffle around. His Shadows stop and the front-facing one starts shouting.

>Did you have to bring us here? The graveyard has bad vibes, and we know you have death issues.

José said, "Quit complaining. Ever since my mother died, I've been working to get over it. You should be proud of me."

The faces shuffled, a loud face at the fore.

>You can't go there. It isn't safe!

Molecular fog and wailing accompanied the request.

José looked back at his Shadows frozen in time. "Stop whining. You're not banshees."

>We don't want to follow you across the graves. Some of the newly dead have issues with connected Shadows.

"So, now you're afraid of ghosts? That sounds a bit ironic."

The Shadows wouldn't move.

>We're not afraid of ghosts. This, though, is different. It's worse, they steal memories.

"You're tough. Fight back. I'll be right here with all the moral support you need."

"We've crossed QTmBits lines before. Use your elbows and squeeze through the line, as you've told me. Don't be such wimps. The dead can't hurt you."

The Shadow's faces continued to shuffle, looking for the right emotion to display. Concern won this hand.

>They can't hurt you. You're not from here. Please wait for the Shadows to melt away.

José turned to his lead Shadow. "Look. I know you. I've had fears like that before, too. All you're doing is picking up on an echo of my old self."

>We don't care. We're not crossing until the grave is sealed.

José thought about it as his Shadows dithered, flipping through their personalities but saying nothing. *I've never acted like this, even when we my* madre *died. Why would my replicants be like this?*

"Fine. I'll go on and you can stay there, unconnected. Maybe we can catch up later and reboot, without meaningless fears, I hope."

The Shadows turn in among themselves, planning, talking, a molecular fog stirring and rising above their one-dimensional heads.

>Alright, we'll follow, but we're not responsible for what happens to your past.

"Responsible for what? There's nothing here we haven't seen or done before."

José picks up his bike and crosses the stream of shadow mourners, giving the core Shadows wide berth, in case his Shadows were right. His line of Shadows fit neatly between the others and follow their host around the grave.

"See? There's no danger. It's just like every other crossing."

His Shadows stutter and pull back. José looks over to see a new Shadow, ghost-like, rising from a nearby grave, embracing one of José's Shadows, dragging it to the ground.

A wave races up and down the line, echoes of fear and pain arcing forward. Every Shadow trembles as the lost soul cries out, a thin banshee wail disappearing in the gray void. The wave front hits José and he starts shaking, a memory is lost and his history broken.

The nearest Shadow flips to an angry face.

>We warned you. Why are you trying to erase your memories?

José sees the multiple faces quickly flip by, including a blank placeholder. *That's disconcerting, at very least*, thinks José. "Sorry, I didn't expect that to happen. Don't worry, I've lots of memories and there are some I'd like to lose. Are you sure there isn't a way to select what disappears?"

>We swear. If you don't respect us, we'll leave and you'll be empty.

"Fine. I'll be more careful."

>And listen to us?

"Yes, yes, just don't bug me. Too many people have tried to tell me what to do and I'm not okay with it."

The mourners on the other side of the TimeWall have all left the grave-site except for one young girl who approaches the gravestone and lays down a flower. She places a small stone on the granite marker. The static line of shadows dipping into the earth wiggles and flips. The host's last shadow, an old woman, moves to the front. The young girls and the deceased Shadows intertwine. The woman reaches out, through the Now and caresses the girl's face.

On the other side of the moving time wall, the girl looks up, touches her cheek as a tear rolls down her face. The shadows tremble and roll back, sliding into the dirt above the grave. The girl's shadow moves away as the Now-girl leaves the site. José steps carefully around the old lady's last shadow and his Shadows give the site a wide berth. No more of his team's Shadows is captured as they move down the path. José lets out a sigh and the leading dozen repeat the sound.

>We're all happy that you're meeting your fears, but please do it on the other side of the wall. You don't understand the repercussions.

"Isn't it your job to teach me?" asked José.

The Shadows flipped faces; it finally came to rest on an older Shadow, almost in tune with his current state.

>Listen, you dolt. We're only representations of your past in a single point of time. We're not alive, but you can destroy us and your memories with foolish actions."

Who does my Shadow think it is, calling me a dolt? "I've never been so insulted. How dare you say that!"

His current Shadow face snorted, gray molecular dust rising with an accompanying rude noise.

>Wrong. You've been insulted a lot worse than this. Shall we call up the chess club incident?"

José shook his head, a tiny memory crept in. "No, please. I don't need to visit all of my past; you can keep it. Hidden deep, if you don't mind."

José jumps on the bike, pedaling fast to leave his memories behind. His Shadows follow, connected with stretched QTmBits.

Chapter 45 -
Time for Styx

Approaching the center of town, José comes across a serious accident. Sirens blend with banshee singing to radiate in the time-space inhabited by José and his entourage.

Smoke merges with Time's gray fog, flashes of fire tearing through the barrier. He sees a couple of young kids milling around the wreckage, one of them is pushing on the TimeWall, looking lost and confused. José's leading Shadow switches to a concerned face.

>Don't you want to help them?

"What do you want me to do?" asked José. "They're stuck where they are. I don't have a map to the River Styx."

The front Shadow insisted.

>Turn on your backpack noisemaker and open the wall.

José hesitated, ready to tell his Shadows all about the tools and abilities of his TimeWall-cracking 'noisemaker' as his Shadow called it, but thought better of it. It was himself, after all, and should know the specifics of the equipment, buried somewhere in his memories.

"And do what?" said José. "It will just prolong the suffering. Best to leave well enough alone. Would you have me running around forcing all the newly dead back to life? Have you thought of the consequences?"

>Here we thought you were a scientist, don't you want to reanimate the dead?

"That is a bizarre question. Are you Shadows, confused about fantasy and reality?"

>Us confused? That's funny, coming from a person walking behind Time. Does all of this look normal to you?

"Okay, I'll admit this is a little weird, but it's real, as near as I can tell."

>Are you sure? Did you bump your head the first time you came here? We did give you a push, remember?

"Ah-ha! That means this is all real, otherwise you wouldn't bring up the past."

>We'll give you that point, but what are you going to do with what you're finding here?

"I don't know. No sensor or photograph seems to make it past the TimeWall. It does make it a little hard to explain to people."

>Great. So you're going to rescue that poor kid?

"No. Except for its entertainment value, what good would it do?"

The new inhabitant of the TimeWorld must have heard José arguing with his Shadows, so he called out and waved.

>He sees you. Are you going to respond?

"I suppose I can't ignore him completely."

>Yes. That would be rude.

"I can jump on my bike, we can be out of here in a flash.

>Rude. Again.

"Okay. I've got it. I'll go talk to him. I hope he doesn't get too upset, being dead and all."

The new inhabitant of TimeWorld kept on trying to get past the TimeWall, as Shadows of his last reality slowly moved backwards.

"Hello," said José. "Do you need any help?"

"Of course, I need help. I can't get to my friends and one of them looks hurt. He isn't moving."

Shadows of the street kept on flowing as Time moved forward.

"My friends are injured and they seem to be distressed. I need to talk to them and let them know I'm alright."

"About that," said José. "You might not be as well off as you think."

"Good to meet you, I don't think we've met before. Do you live around here?"

José's new acquaintance looked around, still a little dazed from his experience.

"What is this place? It smells bad and I don't remember the day being so gray and foggy."

José said, "I'm afraid to tell you that you're dead. It appears that you were in a bad accident and didn't do well."

"That explains the steering wheel I felt going through my chest."

"That would do it," said José

He looked down at his chest. "Next time I'll remember to wear my seat belt."

José's front-facing Shadow shook its head.

"So you're my guide? My name is George. Is this Purgatory? Do I get to travel further?"

"Sorry, that's not my department. I'm not that sort of entity. I'm a TimeExplorer."

"Good to meet you, TimeExplorer."

"I'm José Isaac Davidovich, glad to make your acquaintance. For your information, I'm human, just like you, except I'm not dead, I opened the TimeWall with a machine I built."

"That's interesting, but what should I do? What are these things behind me?"

"Those things are your Shadows. Every moment of your life is encoded in the Shadows. They are you. As to the other question, I don't know what to tell you.

"That's a little hard to believe," said George. "Why would every instance of my life be recorded? Who set this up?"

"It's just the way Time works. It's always moving, and the Shadows are the residue of its transport through space."

His Shadow grunted.

>That is so insulting. We are much more than residue. We have half a mind to report you."

"Report me to who or what?"

George and José waited for an answer. They were met with the soft whining of the banshees.

"As you can see, I'm learning the ropes here, too. I expect you'll want to stay with your body. I've met some unusual characters who are disconnected from Time. I'm pretty sure that isn't a good thing to do."

George said, "You're the expert. I have nowhere else to go and I'm concerned about my friends. Is there any way to contact them and let them know I'm okay?"

"You may be able to do that. I've seen the dead communicate through Time, so it must be possible."

The immensity of his situation was becoming clear to George.

"There's that word again, dead. I don't like the sound of it."

"Nevertheless," said José. "Facts are facts. I need to move along. You'll be fine. Have a good day."

>That was really stupid. He's dead; it isn't going to be a good day.

"Well, what else can I say? This is a very unusual interaction in a very unusual place."

>A place you volunteered to visit, in case you forgot.

José hopped on his bike and quickly left for less contentious locations

As he rode off, José could hear George say. "So, I'm dead, but it's fine. That doesn't sound so good to me."

The ambulance loaded George's old body and drove away, without sirens.

"How am I supposed to follow them? I don't have a car anymore."

Time answered, and George and his shadows were pulled along with the emergency vehicle.

José turned to his Shadows. "Did you know about the transport system? This place is stranger and stranger."

>Of course we knew about it. How do you think we're always where you are, on either side of Time?

"I guess that makes sense. What other tricks do you have that I don't know about?"

>We'll let you know. Now let's get out of here before more people drop in.

"You mean the dead ones?"

>Yes, they sort of creep us out. We're fine with you, but we like our peaceful world.

Chapter 46 -
Time for a Rescue

Before José could continue the discussion of who or what belongs behind the TimeWall, a distant sound caught his attention.

It wasn't the normal decaying noise coming from the TimeWall's direction or banshee singing, but something coming through the distant fog. It was a weak guttural cry, like an animal in distress.

"That's not right. There aren't sounds made behind the time wall unless it's from me or my Shadows. I hope it isn't one of the cryptids the campers warned me about."

There were different sounds, but they were time slices, an indistinct buzzing gray tinnitus of Time noise. Before José could figure out how to stack Time to make it into a playable record he saw a tiny figure in the distance, calling out for his attention.

José thought, *Whatever this is, it's better than dealing with the newly dead. They'll figure it out soon enough - the cemetery isn't too far away I'm sure they'll reunite with their timeline after a while.*

A tiny figure approached, resolving into a biped, stumbling along, dressed in dirty rags.

"Is that Bigfoot? I hope it's friendly. I don't have much food left to share, just a few cookies and the leftover tuna fish sandwich. What if it doesn't like rye bread?"

"Hey, Shadows. What can you tell me about this monster? Do I need to leave?"

>We don't know. There are a lot of strange things back here and we try to keep as far away as possible.

"Once again, my Shadows have proven to be a worthless source of information. I would have thought you would have picked up my thirst for knowledge and spent your idle time exploring."

>Sorry, we're not up to your standards. We could leave.

"Not going to happen, you aren't going to turn me into a zombie. We'll stick together, but I expect you to do better in the future."

>If there is one.

"We're together to the end, whatever that end may be."

I could just take off. I know it can't catch me on my bike. thought José. *I didn't think to bring any weapons. What would even work in this timeless world?*

The ragged cryptic/person got closer, followed by its broken line of Shadows.

Interesting, thought José. *It doesn't look like a Bigfoot, not furry enough. It looks like it's another traveler from the other side of the Wall. Could the university have breached the TimeWall again? It doesn't look like Geoff. I know they would leave someone behind at the blink of an eye, if it was to their advantage.*

The strange biped got closer, and José relaxed a little. It was more human than monster.

"Do I know you?" asked José. The person looked familiar, but the dirty, unkempt beard and slouch hat didn't ring any bells.

"You're José Davidovich, aren't you?" said the slouch-hatted biped. "We met at the Timeless BBQ last year. Don't you remember?"

"Not quite," said José. "There were so many new participants this year. I think they heard about my *madre's* brisket. I hope they weren't disappointed, although my *tio* Carlos cooked up quite a tasty substitute while he was still able to get around."

"I don't know what that's all about," said the newcomer. "But I'm not surprised you don't recognize me. Look, my past is getting chewed up and I can't remember much. You wouldn't happen to know where the TimeWall is located? I'd like to get out of here."

José was careful to keep the TimeWall near and just pointed to his right.

The visitor started walking, then said, "I forgot to ask. Do you have a sandwich? I haven't eaten for a while, think."

"We need to stick together," said José. "Here's half of a tuna sandwich left. I hope you like dill-rye bread?"

He took the sandwich but not the advice, "Thank you so much, kind sir. I'll be leaving you now."

"I don't see a sound generator," said José. "How are you going to open the wall?"

The poor man looked empty-handed and destitute, but José figured if there was a better technology than his huge backpack, he needed to learn about it.

"Oh, that. I guess I lost it when the *Chupacabra* attacked."

"The mythical monster of my youth? I thought those were stories my *madre* and *tio* made up to scare me out of the basement and off to bed. Does everyone else in the world know about the *Chupacabra,* too? Anyway, I don't think a myth can hurt you."

The old man looked askance at José and said, "You better watch out. Monsters will eat your memory. At least I think they can. I'm not so sure at the moment."

"I see you have a broken line of Shadows," said José. "Are you telling me a mythical monster did that?"

"That is no myth, sonny! Now, do you have a way to get out of this mess or not? If you can't help me, I'll be on my way. I'll figure it out myself, thank you very much."

José's Shadows turned and flipped back in time, looking to help their host, checking his past.

>It's Hector. We found the link and you know him.

José realized that his Shadows knew what they were talking about and this was his old friend and mentor. *At least they're good for something,* thought José.

"Hector," exclaimed José. "It's me, your old friend José. Don't you remember?"

Hector looked at José, his backpack and his bicycle and said, "Of course I remember. José, you say? Didn't we meet earlier? You know, I never forget a face. And you're my old friend? Glad to meet you. Now help me get out of here before nightfall when the *Chupacabra* comes out."

José wasn't convinced his friend knew who he was talking to, but felt that he had no choice but to play along. Maybe when he got back on the other side, his mentor's memory would improve. Although looking at his string of missing Shadows, that might not be the case.

Chapter 47 -
Time to Exit

A dark shape came into focus through the distant fog. Walking, sniffing, and looking for something.

"What's that?" asked José. "Don't tell me they have dogs behind the Now. Is it yours?"

"No, "said Hector. "We need leave. *Chupacabra* comes,"

The gray beast began running, bouncing off the TimeWall. Opportunity-time bubbles exploded in bright rainbow colors around the canine-like monster.

"Work faster. He here and wants eat my memory."

José thought, *I do believe he's losing more memories, and a verb or two. I better speak in short declarative sentences, to be safe.*

"It's just a dog," said José. "Don't worry. I have a way with dogs. Let me tell you about Paquito, my mother's Chihuahua. I'm sure he's somewhere along my timeline if you want to meet him."

"I told you. It a *Chupacabra* not a Chihuahua! It dangerous."

"So's a Chihuahua," said José. "Paquito could be mean if he didn't like you."

"Focus," said Hector. "This not a dog and it big and not friendly."

"Okay. Okay. I've got it," said José. "Give me some room to work on my hardware."

José pried open the back and wiggled the batteries. He took them out, filed the tips down and licked them before putting the freshened batteries back in the holder.

"What! You didn't bring spare batteries?" said Hector.

"That's rich coming from someone who lost all of their equipment. Now be quiet, I have to reboot and tune up the generator. I'll need all the power I can find if we're both going to leave."

"*Chupacabra* near, remember?"

José recalled why he and his mentor separated. The guy never seemed to have the time for patience and introspection.

On the other hand, the *Chupacabra* was almost on top of them, every broken opportunity-bubble highlighting its hot breath and timeless eyes. The monster hissed, closing in on its new meal, which looked a lot like José and his Shadows.

>Listen to your mentor. Get a move on, we don't want to be sucked into its belly!

"Calm down, I'm working as fast as I can."

That went over as well as a deflated opportunity bubble. José's Shadows, Hector, and his Shadows were becoming frantic.

"He's got my memory!" screams Hector.

The *Chupacabra* latches onto a molecular wide representation of Hector and shakes it like a rag doll. A gray Shadow disassembles and disappears into the monster's maw. Wailing echoes throughout the dank, fetid air and fades to silence like a cheap, cracked speaker.

Hector grabs José's bike and tosses it at the *Chupacabra*.

"Hey! That's mine, you can't just toss things around that don't belong to you."

"Okay," said Hector. "You go talk to the monster and ask for it back. Now TURN ON your machine!"

Intense wailing of the banshee songs ran up and down the spectrum as his machine warmed up. The edge of time wavered, weakened and split open.

The TimeWall appeared behind the explorers and enveloped them. A crack opens up, then starts to slowly heal, closing the gaping hole.

The *Chupacabra*, with the bike in its jaws, stuck a clawed paw through the self-sealing TimeWall, seemingly waving a fond farewell to its prey.

The hand disappears as time moves forward. A chewed piece of metal tubing, candy apple red with sparkling highlights, clatters to the ground.

"Now look what you've done! I loved that bike and now it's lost to time."

"Do not worry, little boy, I'll buy you another one, with a real wicker basket this time."

José shook his head.

"That was close," said Hector.

"What will happen to my Shadows?" asked José. "Will I lose my memory? What did you do to me?"

"Not to worry. The *Chupacabra* only seems to eat Shadows when the host is around, otherwise it sticks to the freshly departed, especially those who haven't decided which side of the TimeWall they belong to."

"And you know that, how?"

"I've been behind the TimeWall for a while. I observe things. If I had my notepad, I'd show you."

"About that," said José. "What are you going to do now?"

"What I'm going to do is take a bath and change clothes. Do you live nearby? Can you cook?"

José, clearly obligated after saving both their lives, said, "You destroyed my bike. We'll have to walk. You remember how to do that, don't you?"

"Just watch me, youngster."

"And no, I can't cook. We'll have to get some food from the mall," said José

The thought of the campers and their eating habits made mall food even less appetizing than normal.

"Better yet, there's a chicken place not far from here. My treat," said José, thinking. *If they see Hector I'm sure they'll take us for a couple of bums. Anyhow, it doesn't look like he has pockets, let alone money.*

"We have to climb this ridge," said José. "My car is in the parking lot turn-out. Try to keep up."

The pair walked up to the chicken store:

Arizona Broasted Chicken®
'You'll need another napkin'™

"I don't remember this store," said José. "It must be new to the area. It's located awfully close to my regular fried chicken store. It may even be on the same street. I wonder what having more competition will do? I wouldn't mind a price war."

"See?" said Hector. "You've lost pieces of your memory, too. Let's go in. I remember how to eat, at least. Your treat."

"I'd expect no less," said José.

The two Time Explorers, minus their fancy uniforms and regal air, staggered into the chicken palace.

"Sir," said the counter clerk to her boss, "Some more homeless are here and it's almost lunch time. What should I do?"

The manager took one look at the pair and said, "Give them a bucket of chicken and send them outside."

"What if they become insulted when we kick them out and start a fight?"

"Don't worry, I've got this. Watch and learn."

"Welcome," said the manager. "We are running a special and you are the 100th customer today. You've won a bucket of Arizona Broasted Chicken® nuggets. It's takeout only. Is that okay with you?"

José whispered to Hector, "That's good, cause I'm not sure my credit card will work here, something looks off."

"Here's your bucket and extra napkins. Now please leave," said the manager.

José shrugged. The last few days have been difficult and he wouldn't refuse free food, no matter how rude he was being treated.

Hector looked at the bag, "Where's our sodas?"

Cans of *Arizona's Best* carbonated cactus juice were quickly added as the pair were escorted out the side door.

Time continued, surrounding and infiltrating every action as the two explorers struggled up the hill, traveling in the Now, with chicken.

-Time to End -

www.ingramcontent.com/pod-product-compliance
Lightning Source LLC
Chambersburg PA
CBHW020325260626
47156CB00004B/1388